Dream On

Magretch, Chrystos

DREAM ON

Chrystos

PRESS GANG PUBLISHERS
VANCOUVER

CANADIAN CATALOGUING IN PUBLICATION DATA

Chrystos, 1946-
    Dream on

    Poems.
    ISBN 0-88974-029-1

    I. Title.
    PS3553.H57D7   1991   811'.54   C91-091138-X

First Printing March 1991

2   3   4   5   96   95   94   93   92

Cover art © by Chrystos
Editing and text design by Barbara Kuhne
Typesetting and production by Val Speidel
Typeset in Aldus at The Typeworks
Printed on acid-free paper by Hignell Printing Ltd.
Printed and bound in Canada

Press Gang Publishers
603 Powell Street
Vancouver, BC   V6A 1H2
Canada

THIS BOOK IS for all of you courageous readers & listeners
that your lives may be filled with poetry,
especially if you think you hate it

In loving memory of those who left for the other world as I was making this
book—Pat Parker, Mark Waukchen, Sara Altimur & Gary McGill
May their spirits dance on in your hearts as they do in mine

This title came in a dream   I believe if we begin to listen to our dreams,
which are the spirits speaking to us when we aren't as rude as usual, we could
solve many of our troubles   Let us honor our different, sacred paths &
work to transform our anger & grief to change our world so all may live,
without hunger or hatred, in peace

I ask you to join with me in prayer for political prisoners (especially Leonard
Peltier & the D.C. 6) & for the survival with joy of Indigenous Nations all
over the world.

Megwetch

Acknowledgments

THE AUTHOR WISHES to thank the Suquamish & Quileute Nations, where portions of this book were written

I am most grateful to have received a Barbara Deming Memorial Grant, which was helpful at a crucial time

Some of the work in this book was written with the assistance of a Grant in Literature from the National Endowment for the Arts

The author appreciates the support of the following periodicals, where some of this work first appeared: *Diversity: the Lesbian Rag; Lesbian Ethics; Conditions; Fireweed; Sinister Wisdom; Taos Review; So's Your Old Lady* & the anthologies: *Naming the Waves; Intricate Passions; Naming the Violence: Speaking Out on Lesbian Battering*

Gracias, merci, gracias to Arline García for the Spanish translation of "No One Has Gone Before Us"

This book would not have been possible without the tender & fiery support of my lover, Ilene Samowitz
We're not breaking up

Thanks to Korey for keeping my feet warm by sleeping under my desk & wagging your tail at the good ones
Thanks to Sappho, Pusiina & Beast, the cats who think I'm their pajamas
We miss you Boy Kitty
Megwetch to the Eagles, Blue Herons, Gulls, Crows, Wrens & Swallows who arc by my window & keep my mind moving

Contents

WINTER COUNT

By their own report america has killed
forty million of us in the last century
The names of those who murdered us are remembered
in towns, islands, bays, rivers, mountains, prairies, forests
our own names
We have died as children, as old men & women without defenses
We have been raped, mutilated, we have been starved
experimented on, we have been given gifts that kill
we've been imprisoned, we've been fed the poison of alcohol
until our children are born deformed
We have been killed on purpose, by accident, in drunken rage
As I speak with each breath
another Indian is dying   Someone part of our Holocaust
which they have renamed civilization
Our women are routinely sterilized
without their consent during operations for other reasons
I have seen the scars
We are the butt of jokes, the gimmicks for ad campaigns
romanticized into oblivion   So carefully obscured
that many think we are all dead
For every person who came here to find freedom
there are bones rattling in our Mother
The ravage of suburbia covers our burial grounds
our spiritual places, our homes
Now we are rare & occasionally cherished as Eagles
though not by farmers who still potshot us for sport
Suddenly we have religions they want & they'll pay
Down the long tunnel of death my grandmothers cry   *No*
Give no solace to our destroyers
Into the cold night I send these burning words
Never forget
america is our hitler

for PAULETTE D'AUTEUIL & BOB ROBIDEAU

NADIE HA ANDADO ANTES

Nuestros pies tallan cada paso rompiendo hacia el agua nueva
de nuestro espíritu sustento
Alas centellantes al movernos
Nuestros errores reclaman con ojos tristes
Solas están aquellas a quienes no pudimos comprender
En un círculo
cada tazón tiene sentido
Contiene
Bebemos lentamente este aire de nuestras vidas
exprimido cual lágrima soberbia de tierra seca
Difícil es ver con sólo conchas para encender la vía
mientras la luna es un espejo plateado de tierra
que pide lluvia matinal
Nos nutrimos mutuamente con sangre de palabras
gestos en la noche de nuestras diferencias
Una hoguera cada paso
Tal como una navaja nuestro júbilo

Para mis compañeras en *Esta puente, mi espalda*
Traducido por Arline García

NO ONE HAS GONE BEFORE US

Our feet carve each step breaking to new water
sustenance for our spirits
Wings glistening as we move
Our mistakes call out with sad eyes
Those we could not understand are lonely
In a circle
each of our bowls has meaning
Holds
We drink slowly this air of our lives
squeezed like proud tears from a dry land
Hard to see with only shells to fire our way
while the moon is a silver mirror of earth
who calls for morning rain
We feed each other the blood of words
gestures in the night of our differences
Each step a cook fire
Our joy like a razor

for my comrades in *This Bridge Called My Back*

NIGHT VISITS

in clear stars bringing silver corn
her radiance full of memories
ways of those whose bones shape our time
A path opens: My feet are rainbow wolves running
calling a cool song through the caves
down to the crystal blue pool
where I was born softly
My eyes open dark as beginning
There were feathers in a clump in white snow
faint flecks of blood   I felt her hunger
as I passed the startled place of death
rushing over rocks
Bare trees echoed with her loneliness
I was her corn in bad winters
I wanted to be
so much more

for PETER

WHAT DID HE HIT YOU WITH?   THE DOCTOR SAID

Shame   Silence
Not he
She
I didn't correct him
Curled into myself like a bound foot
I looked at the floor ceiling evading
A fist
Hand that has spread me open Fingers I've taken inside me
Screaming   *I love you bitch*   You are the she who rocked
my head side to side
barrier reef for your rage boat
It's safe to beat me
I've lain under your tongue between your thighs
hungry
When I grabbed you to throw you off
you shouted   *If you've scarred my face bitch*
I'll kill you!
I'm sorry   I wept   *I didn't mean to scratch you*
Should have said you won't have a chance to kill me
I'm gonna kill you for thinking you can hit me like that
screaming that you love me
You said   *I haven't hit a woman in 8 years*
8 years bad luck my head caught it
My arms in dishwater scrubbing out my father's shoe
The dream tells me you're familiar
brutality I slide into without a horn
You don't have to be beaten to be loved   the therapist said
I held the cool shock of those words
against the purple bruise of still wanting you
You've hit me with that irresistable
deadly weapon
hatred dressed in the shoes & socks of the words
I love you

MAKING DINNER

Rice peers mysteriously from behind a black satin mask   Cat
provides percussion tongue licking water from the dishes in the
sink   Unwatered plant leans hopefully toward the faucet   She
ignores the pleas   feet which are hungry   Papers which want an
answer   Rose who wants some earth   *She's a bad woman &*
don't you forget it   Distance goes over like cardboard   Inside her
head someone is trying to scratch their way out with a sharpened
spoon   White caps rise like the breath of werewolves   She saw it
long ago   Her uncle came up behind her right as the monster was
coming in the story & scared her teeth out   He gave her
pennies   Not until much later did she know he couldn't have
children because of what grandma had done to him   His eventual
wife couldn't have children either   Hers a car accident that left her
eyes perpetually weeping   Their babies are tossing out there in the
coming storm   A light appears as though to warn   *Get the dinner*
ready   Time to stop daydreaming   seeing visions & terrors
Drink some tea speed up to the real world where people work on their
sailboats earnestly   Pay their taxes & have nothing to do with
Lesbians like you   Her stove is an orange mouth a revlon ad for
glowing lips remembered from her childhood   Rice talks back
boiling over   Grease collects to gossip about her   Sun sets
without fire   Those clouds dull a darker gray   She hopes the
boat will capsize so that in the morning she can read about the
sufferings of the survivors who lost their brave husbands out on a
fishing trip   Not their fish anyway   She wants small terrible
things to happen all around her   She wants to kill the person with
the sharpened spoon   She wants to burn something in a spoon to
kill the pain   Oh no we'll have none of that no more missey   She
wants to find a soap opera which will pull her into the tv & never let
her out   She wants to read lines explaining why she is the way she
is   She wants everything to break up & change in an hour's time
She wants commercials to interrupt her bleakest moments   She
wants a genie in her sink to whirl out & clean all the counters   She
doesn't want to talk to anybody at all for months   Something is
fermenting   She hears the sound of teeth grinding bone   Sound
of tongues in another room   Nobody's really there but she can

hear the arguing   The cupboard doors open soundlessly   The
plates slip out & leave home   can't stand to be treated like this
She feels the empty nest syndrome without having had children
Her beliefs are gone   ideals goals sense that she could matter could
change dust into food   The wind moves indifferently   The boat
doesn't sink   A Gull goes by & mocks her with hoarse cries   *Go
away go away go away from here we don't want you   Can't you
see the red eye of the Dolphin is silent*   In the morning rubies spill
across the floor   She awakens thinking someone is bleeding to
death down the hall   The potholders complain of the cold   The
cups are fighting & bickering among themselves   The machine to
make grilled cheese sandwiches tilts   *Bingo* she wants to shout
bingo bingo   Squash holds down the potatoes & onions   banana
is getting ready to fly to puerto rico & go swimming in the bay
Home it thinks   *take me back home   Too cold here*   Someone
she doesn't know sends a picture of their child with a changed address
She grows darker   Can't see her hands for the forest   Words
words they want to troupe around in elegant formation lure others
with their abilities   She goes off to piss unimpressed   She leaves
blood behind   Teeth are still gnawing bone   The dead trees
under this whisper to her   They're still alive & want restitution
Water rushes through her fingers   The handmade doll from south
america, relic of her lover's childhood, peers from the back of the
shelf   She has pale yellow silk panties   She's made of carefully
hoarded scraps stitched probably by an Indian woman maybe a maid
like me in big white houses where silk swoons in the afternoon with a
headache   Needs mint tea & absolute silence   Hungry lover will
be coming home soon   Dark & cold bite into the house which leers
at the cliff below   Perhaps an earthquake will slide everything out
to sea & she won't have to wash it   She forgot to call last night
now it may be too late   she wasn't ready anyhow   it doesn't
matter while hurting in a dry place where her not belonging here
     not being ready   not having time   all sit around & criticize
her   As the rice cackles if only that Lesbian who can never find the
screwdrivers or the butter has left one here   Next year I'll produce
all the screwdrivers tied together with a long leather thong & call it
art   Sell it back for something foolish   Heavy breasts will want
to know what she has been doing all day   Impossible to explain

that getting through the glue sometimes takes that long & arguing
dinner into submission has a special exhaustion   Could she claim
to have rescued the men in the boat after scrambling down the cliff &
almost falling   Better look in the recipe box there's bound to be an
excuse in there   at least find a worried sad face to dredge in
flour   That answer: *Nothing*   carries no weight

DEAR INDIAN ABBY

What should I do
about those ones who try to crawl down my throat
bulging eyes are going to Understand
me or Else
Get some of my spirit   get some of my magic
OOOOOHHHHHHHOOO they want it
Want to explain how I could have a better grasp
of Native issues if I read this book or that by some
white person   Want me to listen to them with traps
dangling from their back pockets
Gonna get some   gonna get some of me now
from *Sincerely Puzzled*

Dear Puzzled, Best thing to do is tell them you've heard
there's a great Indian wise woman named Whale Rabbit
over anyplace around 3,001 miles away
& you're real sure
she's waiting patiently for them to show up
& they'd better hurry cause her fee goes up in 2 weeks
& your fee for giving them the directions is only $350
Don't forget to smile
as you wave goodbye
Yours Truly, Indian Abby

ACRYLIC FOR LEE

We were swimming in the public pool her cropped hair
a dead giveaway in girls & boys land where fingernail polish
reigns supreme
She'd offered to drive me regularly because it helps
my bad back & I don't have a car
We came to rest at one end as the others splashed laps
Half afraid of my own question I asked
Are we friends yet or is it still too early?
She looked hard into the water answered
Yeah, it's too early
& swam off
Later as we dressed we glanced shyly at each other's bodies
didn't admit it
not from desire but curiosity   Our lovers were once lovers
so here we are
juxtaposed naked & wet & trembling for all the clean cut
american reasons connected with swimming pools
neither of us in the least american
her darkness Lithuanian mine Menominee
Our lovers fair freckly pink & white with green eyes sandy hair
They lived together for 8 years
On this
& swimming every afternoon we're attempting
to build a friendship which shows constant signs of drowning
for lack of training
It pains me that she had to get a dog to speak her language
because her family have cut her off for being Queer
I don't even know
my language   My father wouldn't speak it having been beaten
silent in boarding school
I've looked in musty volumes of natural history
for the ancestors under the water of my memory
She drinks too much beer or gin when they have the money
I write
it's the same thing a sloshing of words against that loneliness
special to those with no home an erased & bloody path

We made her a stained glass elephant for her birthday
She wept   I wept at her tears
which we both hid
It seems making her a beautiful window has helped
If I was painting our portrait I'd concentrate
on illuminating the negative space with strange designs
in brilliant colors   Our eyes would be averted
but our hands would touch
as though by accident & the closeness
of the frame which pushed us unrelated
together

especially for LEE MARYTE

PRIORITIES

When he asked me the time
I said   *Don't bother me*
I'm thinking of a beautifull woman

Ignoring my lack of watch
he grew angry
I put his anger in a passing trash can

I am still
thinking of a
beautifull woman

for MARTINE PIERRE-LOUIS

HE HAD A VISION

that he should share the pipe with whites
to save the earth
She told us this
after saying that her grandfather was the episcopal minister
at Pine Ridge who fuels the anger of Vine Deloria
The man with the vision told the circle
Here is the pipe   It will connect you with the earth
Do not smoke it unless you seek this connection
She smoked
Now she feels this connection   expands
I ask his name so I can give it to other whites
who want me to share my spirituality
as I refuse
He has connected her   Given her back the earth
She doesn't even remember his name

for RENÉE PERRY, who helped me keep my temper

SOFT

breasts of fire we live on the water my tongue
drinks you   Wind comes through your tender thighs
I am shaken   You moan the sun changes   Smoke whips
through the air burning on the water   You are a woman who
holds me   Could become warm sky here   Fish between
your legs gasp for air   We share a good meal
Cook pots full on the water one can see far into the wind
The crying sky changes my tongue whips you burning
I am a woman turning you in my arms like air
holding warm smoke delicious   Your need holds
secret wind   My fingers reach for your burning sky
You are the place of sweet water my hands drink
My breasts on your belly   Place where burning becomes
Time fishes for new water moaning
A place where each stroke could be as slow
as breathing smoke   Your belly makes circles of pleasure
on the water   Opening I gasp for life
Clear place where water & fire meet   Moan of wind in my hair
you could touch me & light a fire
My hands hold you a bouquet of lush
flowers on fire   Tall & stately my tongue
takes you down
to the water where we live

INTERVIEW WITH THE SOCIAL WORKER

It all started because I gave her my best chair
with the black velvet cushion
embroidered with red roses
& she sat in it like it was a disease
She said   *How can you live like this*
I said   How can you live like that
she said   *Don't get smart with me*
I said   I'm always smart I have too many brains
it's not my fault   genetics
She said   *I don't think you're eligible*
I said   I'm still unmarried   she said
That has nothing to do with it I think
I am through here
I said   I'll never let you through here
Not if I have anything
to say about it

ONE DAY DREAMING

someone silver I knew came to whisper
Grandmother of everybody who swims in water
she said   *Clearly*
fish cannot belong to someone who will mount us on a board
Unnatural not to eat
what one kills
It is the law of life
Certainly your people & my people lived in harmony
for thousands & thousands of years
before those loud ones showed up
We never had to be managed or farmed or hatched
Your prayers were all we needed
Now the waters in every place grow dark with strange murk
We've watched them throw the most amazing things overboard
as though our home is their toilet
Sometimes even things someone smarter could use again
Swimming around in my hair I hear her call
Keep fighting them
Keep praying for us

in Honor of DAVID SOHAPPY & all the People of the River

JET COLOR LAB

After five years of sharing a bed our breasts meet accidentally
in the photo shop after our mouths don't speak for three months
Hello Jane
You answer   *Hello*   looking intently at the blank wall
Negative space whirls us   The clerk a mute witness
to our throbbing hands   cramped feet   cropped memories
It was not long enough
It was too long
The black formica counter breathes & recedes
Hello Goodbye your shoulder is familiar but I can't
place your heart which negates all
I was to you   You ride a new woman whose photos you bring
through the rain which meets my tears unexpectedly
I huddle wet for your comfort but you come down slick
cement steps without pausing
I'm witness to your sharp indifference
mute fingers of our life reach to touch your face
which is as close as those thousand mornings
when we rode through love so carelessly
Later I glance in a mirror of ice to see how I looked to you
My eyes are a wall that won't speak to me

BRIGHT IN YOUR DARK MOUTH

your tongue sliding along your lips pink
as you lick words
Thoughts drift across your face
You're telling me of the woman you want
fighting to walk off the ruts you've known
I watch your tongue
your eyes where I could glide in
my body a glimmer in their black luster
You're onyx   a molasses woman
tall with muscles on your back   long feet
You dance on coals
You speak of her   I watch you
my lips drifting through a seduction scenario
where I polish your skin until you reflect light
Your pink tongue tending mute places in my body
wants to cradle yours
I sit on my hands to stop from cupping your breasts
as your shirt leans open
We embrace goodbye   good friends
Your mouth still wet with crumbs of her
mine wet
with wanting your pink tongue to speak to me
without words

WAKING UP

next to a ten foot high mound of garbage sacks in a crash pad with rats running over my feet was the moment which pierced me like the sun coming through a broken window which seemed about a mile away but even then I knew was only a few feet   In the haight, a converted old victorian with a white enamel sink unit across from me full of burnt back spoons, candle stubs & vomit

Frightened of the rats but too stoned to move   Trying to get my hand to scratch my nose for a long time   HiJack was beside me, he'd pissed his pants again   Some other people I didn't recognize in the shadows, maybe Harold my old pimp & his mother who was still working the streets   Didn't get much anymore   Though still breathtakingly pretty with huge green eyes in a dark gold face Used to go with Harold for his mother not him   I'm sure I'm the only one still alive from that moment

Didn't get straight then not for another year or so but that was the knife of knowing I had to

Later that day I tried to get HiJack to screw me on a mattress with mice nesting in it but he couldn't get it up   I wasn't horny, men didn't satisfy me, but I wanted a connection a root I wanted to know I could move, was more than a blissful sack of garbage

We went to a burger place on fillmore   The Black lady who owned it & did the cooking knew we were junkies but fed us anyway if she got her money up front   No problem HiJack had plenty   His southern parents mailed him checks to stay away   He had accidentally murdered a Black man in a street fight & he couldn't get over it   Nobody sent him to jail of course & his parents were furious that he felt guilty & bad   He was supposed to act right & not care   I think he dumped me after he told me the truth which no one else knew   He was too afraid they might kill him   Afterall who would care if they did   He cried in my arms sobs that catch my breath still   His favorite song was Strange Fruit which he used to sing off-key until I wanted to hang him

I was so dependent & stupid then   thought I had to "have a man"
or I'd be killed   The next one was from the midwest & tall   I
noticed the change in accents   That's all I remember except for a
night when we slept on clothes pulled from salvation army bags in
someone's basement he broke into   She came down to do the
laundry very early & we scrabbled like rats to get out of there as she
screamed at us,   *Filthy Bums!*   over & over   I can hear her
voice now   She probably rewashed the whole pile

Taken me over twenty years to write this, to stagger away from my
shame, to form letters that say: this is who I was   I escaped my
family to the streets   thought I had it made   I don't think *Filthy
Bum* when I see anyone living on the street   Could be me
Could be you   What I ran from seemed far worse that what I ran
to   There's worse I can't write yet maybe never   echoes of our
feet in alleys   breakfast at missions listening to bug-all about
jesus   faceless men I sucked   This voice has been dragged from
sleeping with garbage, this voice, my voice, has terrible stories I'm
afraid of   Worst hallucinations are rats chasing me to get a bite
sometimes they do   Time was I had nothing but rage & grief & my
wits   Now I seem to have more, to be safe, hold jobs, carrying
silently within that one breath away from *Filthy Bum*

for those who are clean, for those who will be & for those who won't make it

THERE ARE PICTURES

of white children & adults holding
Fox   Otter   Elk   Coyote   Bear Cubs   Wildcat Pups
in their arms like teddy bears   Nuzzling the fur
their ancestors ruthlessly slaughtered
This happens at the olympic game farm daily except mondays
Behind the people   slightly out of focus
are rows & rows of three-foot by three-foot wire cages stacked
where these unstuffed animals are kept
between sessions of hugs
You could say
maybe these animals would be dead if they weren't such good
all-star entertainment
Maybe it is fine
to turn life into a cloying hallmark card
Maybe the animals are happy
like this
Looking at their cages
I doubt it
Looking at the people I am so sad for them
their clinging arms hope for affection
from Beings
so much deeper & more alive
than that

for THERESA CORRIGAN

DEAR MARY FRANCES

I live in an inaccessible house on a steep hill it was all
we could afford
The restaurant where we ate last night has only one step
but the ladies isn't accessible   There was a man in a chair
I asked him if maybe the men's was   He said he didn't plan
on finding out he was used to it
The last reading I did was in a completely inaccessible
place, a flight of stairs nobody could even fake it
I forgot to ask beforehand, I'd never been there, I'm fighting
so many battles at once & losing most   I mentioned it during
the reading maybe next time they'll do better
My old landlord made me dismantle the ramp I put up
because he said if I wasn't in a wheelchair myself there
was no excuse for it   I was too scared of being evicted
to fight back I was used to that place
I've hardly been anywhere since I saw you last that is
acceptable   I lost the tapemeasure I was carrying around
to argue with
I hope this *Bless Me Mary Frances I Have Sinned* routine
doesn't piss you off I just wanted you to know that you're
not alone & I'm not going to give up & get
used to it

for MARY FRANCES PLATT

34

CLEAR SPHINX

of time in my dreams
Sappho your black gaze of centuries holds
every woman who has loved women
lain beside breasts in the sweet
slow water of our song
I see myself refracted a million colors
stars falling in the deep wheel
unbroken
by their flames   their accusations   their deaths
I cry your name unafraid
for we are sacred
consecrated to clarity
Our palms ripe mirrors
which bear the fruits
of our mouths

MY PLACE

I am the woman whose full arms carry wood to your fire
in the dark
My pulse whispers your name   wind like doeskin
through the trees
I am the woman who stirs your food
watching bubbles turn to stars
I am the woman kneading your days
putting your dreams out to rise in warm bowls
I am the woman who weaves you a marriage sash
my hands purring
I am the woman who wets your mouth
whose silence moves you to another world
My back a rainbow trail
My voice a coyote howl
My feet falling leaves

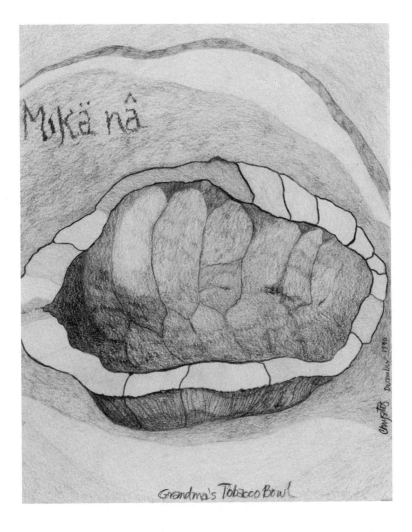

Mukä nâ

Grandma's Tobacco Bowl

AT THE MOON GATE

Chinese restaurant I heard a blonde woman say
with an appalling sneer
Oh she's ugly
She has to take
whatever
she can get
I don't
Her husband replied
through a mouth full of sizzling rice soup
That's true
with a certain proud satisfaction
Later she snarled at her maybe five-year-old daughter
We'll never take you out
again
if you don't sit like a child
instead of a dog
I am praying for this small one
asking the Moon
to protect her
Later my fortune said
Kindness is the greatest wisdom

IN HER I AM

fine dark pulsing without time where I'm meant to be
Clear well fed no words calculating next move
No misunderstanding this muscle which breathes with my hand
enfolded hot as air vibrating in summer
Slurping my tongue is a cat feather river vortex
an angel night jasmine wind licking us clean
We're hurtling through stars becoming
here
as we so rarely are
Heavy with longing to stir ourselves from ember to embrace
Moaning with you so deeply in you I'm no more than air
to meet your need
Sobbing rocks fly through my heart in a river that breaks
down into my eyes where closed & black I am suddenly
red & searing hot rubies

ALONE

in the Queer bar with ice water that cost $1.50
twenty years & hundreds of girlfriends later
I still
don't know how to do this
Never will
So I enjoy the closely swaying women's bodies
flicker of simmering desire
in this one place where we can sort of be
ourselves
that in every town is always smoky, tacky & not quite clean
where class & race dim somewhat in red spinning lights
a haze of booze
Sober
this is not my home
but there's no place else to go
in a strange city

SOMEWHAT

over five years later I stand in my garden holding
a postcard addressed to you forwarded
from a cottage where we haven't lived in seven years
sent by a fancy store on fifth avenue where I've never been
You
& I don't speak
It came a few days ago   can't throw it out   may be all
that's left of what was us
I notice you can
still bring tears to my eyes as I crumple
your name in a tired ball
This card arrived at our first funny crooked home where I
was full of hope   roses   planting tomatoes   raising chickens
a Japanese garden we created
smell of our breasts sleeping together
I thought we were happy   my happiness
obscured your discontent which leaked through walls
I notice now in retrospect
Crossed out several times in a strange
hand as I have tried to erase you in conversations
with strangers this card arrives here
in my home
where you have been once when mutual friends betrayed me
by bringing you & your new lover who had almost been mine
to a party in which I laughed a lot so you wouldn't know
how I couldn't stand to see you laughing without me
I remember that little house where I broke my back
when attic studio stairs disintegrated under my feet
& I fell
Was that our undoing
Long months of pain when I wasn't anything but staying alive
dragging from one doctor to another   finally surgery
more long pain when I couldn't remember the movie we'd seen
the night before   Scars that echo still
I was your icon of strength freedom wildness
fecund earth mother although I thought you just loved me

How many times you bragged to strangers that I had & could
survive anything   I didn't survive our separation
though I'm still alive
When I broke you didn't know what to do tried everything
I've called our memories back from the mountains
I've washed your name from my hands
for longer than they touched you
I've stared into grief until I went numb
These tears are speaking to your harsh heart
heart I scarred
with my rage at your repeated betrayals   bland denials
Escada: A Trunk Showing   it says   I've heard of them
$669 blouses   No wonder you gave a false address
Did you ever tell me the truth I'm dragging up the buried dead
with a screech I muffle quickly away from here
I can imagine you wandering in there on a bored lunch hour
& when pressed for your address
scribbling down an old
well-remembered one with the certainty
that it would never arrive
We lived in another house after our first one & I've lived here
without you as separation has carved me deeply
The island postal system remembers our connection
though we deny it
The same Anna who brought our letters to lytle road
& mountainview drive comes here with mine
You probably don't remember her she is the kind of ordinary
person you ignore or cutting closer
don't even notice
She & I wave smiling at the grocery store / I leave her cookies
I've baked at christmas or valentine's   give her roses
from this garden if I'm out when she comes by
She assumed I'd know where
you are
Thinking of you I go to tackle blackberry roots the worst kind
tenacious & cutting   Still easier than planting
a new life without reference to our cruelty
Will I ever finish these excavations after the fact while

you gaze off in the distance for something more interesting
to do
Did you do this
on purpose
To keep your stick stirring old coals
I'm sure you know how deep my burns
though possibly wired into your own
you think me indifferent & poke
looking for the root back into my heart
Could I send you a telegram
Please Use A San Francisco Address When Shopping Stop
I throw out this postcard
change the tape from music I gave you   Put dry dishes away
You ate from some of them
I've not touched you at all
since the last time we made love
Watch out that root
is a live wire

for JANE

THE BORDER RAZOR

At u.s. customs nervous I know I'm going to be inspected
because the rich american white couple in front of me
match every nice tourist ad you've ever seen
& the line behind me is all white
so I stick out like a sore red thumb after the hammer misses
Holding my breath even though I know it makes it worse
I move forward juggling sleeping bag, old jacket, worn
suitcase & overflowing shopping bag
He wants my driver's license & punches me into his computer
I panic
He reads for too long giving me too much time to wonder
if a radical Indian activist can cross the border
or an ex-mental patient or someone with a dusty
but served jail record
I can't remember if Lesbians are illegal
Finally with a reluctant shrug & a piercing stare he lets
me go
still suspicious he watches me stagger back to the bus
I wonder how long until the time when I'll be kept
& if I can speak
what I'll say in my defense

INDIAN CARS

she said laughing   *Indian cars are special sometimes*
there's no floorboards or the doors don't shut & you have
to be real careful
you don't fall out
One of her cars was called Buckskin Two because a lot
of it was held together with leather thongs
My car is a rare '72 toyota with at the moment only
two cylinders going until I get the money to fix
the head gasket
but she can still do fifty on the freeway if I need it
She has absolutely beautiful moss growing on her sides
in various hues of green   Her name is Jimmie Lee
after the first woman I fell in love with when I was
about seven or eight   She is Navajo & had hair in a river
down her back which later her children nagged her into
cutting off so she could be more modern & I cried
while my mother was angry with me for being such a fool
Sometimes the horn goes off by itself
I think she's warning the Deer who cross the road
staring at me while I stop & wait for them
as they ripple slowly to nibble over in the state park
their eyes quiet as sacredness

for ELIZABETH WOODY

SHE WAS THERE

against warm cement walls as my bus slowed
It was her place
she defended   fierce warrior
hissing with no saliva at the white folks going by
her hatred a deep & terrifying pool
where I see my own heart often caught
She was more *there* than anyone else on the street
a moving gesture against high heels / nobody "seeing" her
cement / carbon monoxide / not a leaf anywhere / workers
in their suits marching from lunch
Hissing at it
the whole scene
everything
How can I bring her life into your hearts
vivid as her blue
knit cap, red sweater, galoshes?

for JACKIE MOOREY

JUST LIKE YOU

I get a lot of junk mail
I read mine because I don't have a tv
Today the american eagle outfitters catalogue arrived
for spring
Now I have many complex bitter feelings about the words
american & Eagle in conjunction but I opened
to the first page anyway where in romantic patagonia
four spray-starched ken & barbie dolls are leaning
on a stone balcony against a mountain backdrop
The women are looking sophisticatedly hostile
in another direction
One blond boy smiles into nothingness
while the brunet one has his head tilted
toward the brunette woman in an attitude of tender
indulgence which you never see in life
Brunette's feet are bare despite snow in the background
she had matching rosy pink polish with no chips
on all her nails
These icons are so clean
wear bright blue, red & yellow
are ready to go sailing on someone's rosewood & brass yacht
any minute
To the left of this beach ball collage
are four brown-skinned women
Their hair is uncombed
They are touching one another huddled
three have bare dusty feet
Their clothes are brown, black & white
the buttons are crooked
The oldest woman, perhaps twenty
has a baby bundled on her back
These are the only brown people in the whole catalogue
I'm sure they were unpaid
The only person looking straight at the camera
is a small girl, eight or nine
who is sitting on the stone like a buddha

She's wearing a large tan felt man's hat with a straight brim
that comes down almost over her eyes
Her shoes are old & split   you can see her toes peeping out
In her hands is a slingshot with the strap drawn back
She looks as though she'd like to put a rock
right through the camera lens
just like me

GETTING DOWN

to the bone place where blood is made
and every moon's a mother
your hands & tongue
in me a brush fire I wake up wanting you
Shrill cry of a dawn bird between my legs
memories of your sweet brown breasts
brushing my thighs
You go
where no one
has gone before until I'm weeping laughing
as you murmur in my wet ear
your husky voice like hot blood   *I love you*
My hair in your mouth burns for you
your lips nibble my lips my breasts
think they can't live without you
Between moments of you I'm a bird
who flies out of vision
You come
like the first bird breaking open the night with dawn
stars bursting into day sucking you I'm made
a moon sweet with light
Crying in the bone & blood place where you make me
yours

for JOANNE GARRETT

IN THE RITZY

where they have the tallest & fattest flower bouquets
in the world & a live cocktail piano tinkling illusions
the chic white faggot headwaiter with perfect face
perfect fingernails & suit to match
concealed imperfectly his fastidious racism
hardly able to keep his hands from flicking
imaginary flies off our heads
seated us in the remotest corner of the patio
which is what we wanted anyway
away from the other diners white & shocked
by our long dark Indian hair in a public place
we shouldn't be able to afford
while we laughed
had three beers between the four of us
His eyes lifted at what he was sure was our drunken
rowdiness when we weren't drunk
as he carried a whole magnum of champagne
to a white table for one as though
it were a precious offering
We enjoyed ourselves despite a sparse dinner
too expensive for the quality
without saying anything to each other
about the ooze around us
Later we decided not to go back
as we all had severe indigestion

BARGAINING

You're in my teeth gritty
all the times I'm sweet
& all the times you don't pay me back with sweetness
hoping the exchange will even out
Doesn't
pitted like my skin I gave you / you gave me / I gave you
somehow it never balances
Builds into a sharp pile of rage longing
We fight about who has the right to be angriest
hurling accusations in a street brawl of words
We trade fury
calculating values / hunger / cold
I forgive in order to be forgiven
You offer your mouth in a gesture of hope
We keep saying   *I love you*
those savage words of greeting
but this isn't love
it's a flea market

ECONOMICS 101

Let's face it
nobody wants to talk about this
but pimps are scum
johns are scum   tricks are scum
& prostitutes can still make more money
than a secretary or a teacher or a nurse or a welfare worker
Johns support the pimps support the johns
passing bucks back & forth across many colored palms
Women are small change in the war of the sexes
Most prostitutes were molested as children
I used to think   *Hey if they're gonna take it anyway*
might as well make 'em pay for it
If you're thinking some generals in south america
have some torture you don't wanna hear about what some johns
did to me or to Pat or to Crystal
All I'll say is
I still can't wear tampax twenty years later
You must be crazy if you thought I could find protection
from bad johns by reporting them to the cops
because some of the worst ones ARE cops
I was lunch hour trade in the financial district
I'm all in favor of decriminalizing prostitution
The trouble is I want to jail all the pimps
& jail all the johns which would wreck business
& I don't mean just ours
There's still no work to replace selling your mouth
or your cunt or your breast or your ears for cheap therapy
which may be all you've got
to sell in this great american cesspool of a dream
If you're Native or Black or anybody not Miss White
you may not be able to get
any other work
I already know you don't want to hear about all the resumés
my friends submit & how hard they try
to get jobs
but some of the feminists will still tell you

it's your fault
& why can't you see
that those johns are scum & those pimps are scum
& somewhere or everywhere you must be hurting like hell
to do this
You'll notice they don't have a job lined up for us
with comparable pay
We could laugh & say   *Hey your daddy or your brother*
was just over here
Why don't you go talk to him, get a mr. grant or two
Hand it over to me & then I'll talk to you but I'm busy
right now
We could say   *Hey give me a job teaching women's studies*
because I know a lot more than you
about being a woman
or we could say
Listen buy yourself a short tight red dress & shoes to match
Work the tenderloin one night
& if you live
Come on back
& we'll talk about scum all night if you want

ON THE BUS

full of anybody else but Indians
I called out
Hey there's an Eagle
They all looked
& for a heartbeat you could feel
their awe
then fast as a microwave
they recovered their frozen dinner faces
& looked at me like I was really
crazy
so from now on
I'm keeping all my Eagles to myself

for RAVEN

I WAS MINDING MY OWN BUSINESS

on the ferry when a white man with distinguished silver hair
in a gray pinstriped suit & cigar just called me
ugly
for no reason at all
as I walked past him
on my way to the toilet
I lashed back   *I'd rather be ugly than stupid!*
Get out of my way!
which was dumb to say but they always catch you
with your pants down
your mind on other things
He had the nerve to say   *My good manners*
prevent me from saying that to you
I should have punched him a good one in the gut
Everyone was staring at raised voices
I didn't dare hit him
because they were all white & impeccable too
Between my black sweatshirt with a hole in one elbow
& his tailormade wool
who do you think would go to jail?
Between my job as a maid & his ordering others around
who do you think the judge would listen to?
Between my arrogance & his
who is right?
He may well be the husband of somebody I've cleaned for
The other day a husband referred to me as a
character
with scorn in his voice
when I called his wife
his hand not quite covering the receiver
probably deliberately
Heart pounding tears turn to rock crystal

Spasmodically I clench & unclench my fist
body shaking
it's a good thing I'm going dancing
I hope
I don't spend weeks hearing his voice & feeling ugly
The good manners in this country
are enough to kill you

for LEE & DENNIS MARACLE

THIRTEEN WAYS OF LISTENING TO CROWS

1)
AWWRRack arrwakk   they laugh from the driftwood fence
as I pull
stones & roots from the umber earth of the garden

2)
Black sky of wings before the mountain blew
they announced lava to come
& ash that would drift over our new lime lettuce

3)
Down at the shore a fight with creamy Gulls
over Smelt raining
froth of coral roe in the surf
Suddenly Eagle swoops / snatches
raucous complaints
silence

4)
In very high blue
tail of Eagle chased by a pair of angry Crows:
stolen egg

5)
Satisfied
pecking the roof with claws curled over the edge
a single Crow tilts an eye to watch me
so small below
Nods / flys
Her wings whisper in the morning dew

6)
Getting out of a tired taxi
grimy with airports, bad food, hostile strangers
Crows up in the red madronas
are the first sweet sound

7)
Walking like an egyptian the Crow discos
near the blooming blackberry field

8)
Awakened by the yellow beak
of the Crow
I yawn

9)
Out on the Rez where the Crows shiny shine shine
rainbows on their backs
they don't move as you go by
too fat to say a word

10)
When I knew you were dying & couldn't get down there to say
goodbye
Crows sat in the apple tree eating nits from their wings
I thought for sure I heard them say
Naoooo Nawwoooo Nooooo

11)
In new winter rain Crows huddle on the shed
staring down into the empty garden so mournfully
I relent & bring out crackers to scatter
AHH haa haa ha   they call like old movies with keystone cops

12)
She writes that she shoots at the Crows
I hear a sob in the back of my throat
that sounds like a Crow

13)
That morning you left for good
I burnt the tortillas four times
Crows cackled with glee as I tossed broken bits on the grass
Their pleasure made me laugh
it's how I survived

in Honor of R. CARLOS NAKAI

ONE FOOL TO ANOTHER

When the owls called to us we rode through a breaking
dawn sky   Beadwork patterns racing between our fingers
Our hands spoke when the small birds sang so sweetly
closing our long night of stones   words   memories
women in common   You entered with a soft feet spirit
We called to one another in voices of owls
We called to one another in morning songs
I heard the tree branch shake a bouquet of snow to the ground
both of us far from home
We rode to where I live   to the Three Sisters Mountains
to deep green hills where you live
to stones we leave behind
We called to owls from our horses
We called to the snow
to the indigo sky
We were so beautifull
everybody thought
the sun was rising

for BONNIE JO PRICE

HOMESICK SONG

Illusive as the color of water I become clear
The red buoy rocks in the salmon run
Where the tide goes farthest out water becomes a mirror
Kelp glitters   Many birds squeal & cry
they call explosions of a distant mountain
white waves answer willingly
Mystery of the shore speaks her own language
of broken shells   pottery shards   debris
I move slowly still as driftwood unraveling
this gray blue day   My steps translate
sand into relatives
Sharp glass speaks of hunger
arms with no one to hold
Everyone
is a long way from here
across a sky with no path

for BARBARA CAMERON

HE BURNT

a swastika on her grass
He was drunk   he said he didn't know
that her family died in the nazi Holocaust
burning through the sod   Cries of burning bodies
children whose hollow eyes are caught briefly
in old newspaper photographs being loaded to die
Music burnt   Philosophy burnt   Memory burnt
burning through us the stench of kerosene
Could we continue
to live there
digging up the black remains near rose bushes
Always that grass will have a faint trace
unless it is entirely dug up & replanted
Every morning as her children go to school
she glances there with a burning shudder
putting sandwiches in bags
She remembers her mother's memories
of Rosa   Sarah   Claire   Hannah   Nora   Ruth   Judith
She remembers their flight to south america
where the nazis followed
when it seemed they had lost
Their symbol covering jackets of teenagers on street corners
my eyes burn   I know the nazis won
as the slaveowners have
We see the evidence of their victories
in every morning's paper burning with a stench
that fills our lives
Not so long ago some other boys burnt a cross
on the grass of a Black family
less than thirty miles from the grass of my home
I have dead I carry of my own
I'm sorry   he said   *I didn't know what I was doing*
Oh but
he did

INCEST KEEPS ON KEEPIN ON

pushin my shoppin cart of rocks
to that dragon of love leanin against a wall
clear & dark
I can't eat what's on sale   my back hurts
lost my shoes   give any girl
skin off my back   hands   mouth
I'm your average pushy dyke stud lookin for legs to spread
thinkin it'll get me a free meal   soft bed   home
for a moment until a blonde comes along
Glass is cracked   rain leaks in   my tongue throbs
Aching beatup tin heart pushed aside
I'm buying time
have rocks in my head   breasts   cunt
Don't ask me to love you
I only know how to lay you / hate you / please you
underbelly I learned from twelve to twenty-one
lyin under him lyin
pushin his rocks off me / in me / down my throat / up my ass
this hurts is dark deeply embedded
sell me a little solitude   self-respect   surprise
Humpin you is my way to forget
it's
all I know how to do

for ROSIE DIAZ

I MUST ADMIT

the highpoint of my cross-country tour by train
was the absolutely delicious moment
when the conductor pointed out to the perfectly
groomed, expensively-suited, clean-shaven, well-educated
white man in front of me
that he was on the wrong train
going in the opposite direction
& could not get off
until wilmington delaware
which we would reach about 3 a.m.
where no other trains would be leaving until seven
& the hotels would probably be shut down for the night
This moment
rests in the matrix of my running for trains I just barely
made in los angeles, albuquerque, chicago, pittsburg , new york &
philadelphia because I don't wear a watch
because they don't work on my body
because I'm fascinated by the women driving me to the stations
which they didn't always know where they were
or how bad traffic would be
In addition, my luggage doesn't match, I forget to comb
my hair because I'm so tired & I can't stand to dress up
to sit around uncomfortably especially when I know I'll
probably drop part of my terrible tuna sandwich on my clothes
as I try to eat it jerking along still mad about having to pay
$2.75 for wonder bread with a lot of stale celery & too much
mayonnaise
Don't forget that I ask six or seven people in the line & station
before I ever board
if this is the right train to wherever
& worry until I actually arrive about whether they're all
tricking me

I treasure that poor man who never even looked flustered
for a moment when he left at 3 a.m. with his luggage initialed
ICK
I derailed myself from speculation on what his name could be
& whether it was an inside joke
because surely if your initials really are ICK
you wouldn't use them
Of course he hasn't spent his entire life being called a
dumb Indian, a stupid girl, an incompetent fool or any
of the other beasts that roam my spirit continually
so he can afford
to make a mistake

fondly, for DELLA MCCREARY

COMING BACK TO AMERICA

the pinched white lady
remarked sotto voice to another one
The bathrooms here are very NICE
with a busload of implications riding her tongue
as though all of canada teems
with cockroaches, virus, mold, ants, spiders & especially
filthy foreigners
I couldn't stop myself from saying that I'd noticed
how clean canada was in comparison to seattle
Her answer a sniff
that could have dismissed an army of us
filthy Indians

NA' NATSKA

Teasing your eyes flicker like tongues on my lips
little roses your nipples become red mountains
My tongue climbs into you
shaking our legs sweat sliding
Your fingers in me are ruby-throated
humming birds   Your eyes iridescent wings
Deep I open   my stomach rises to meet your hands
wet with me   I suck your fingers
You laugh a gurgle of nectar
We go shining in the rainy road your palm kneading
my thigh   mine yours
I murmur   *Am I affecting your driving too much?*
Tossing your head smiling you answer
I want you to
All day I'm wet as I paint
while you study falling asleep after twenty-six pages of greek
I roll in you like first snow melt shocking my blood
with this glistening new
river of humming birds between us

for ALICE FISHER

I LIKE TO THINK

of the Black miners in south africa
continually
I like to remember that they are always
Black
& always inspected thoroughly as they come from the mines
bringing gold   silver   chrome   diamonds
for always white owners
I need to remember their wages
aligned with the price of diamond & gold jewelry
& so do you
I need to know
they plunder what is their own land
I like to think about the days they spend in total darkness
about how long it is before they see their wives & children
I like to remember the misery of death
under the gleam of necklaces   rings   cars   knives   spoons
I like to think of how much we have in common
stripping our lands for the master
I like to remember all the white owners
of Navajo rugs   Zuni jewelry   Lakota shirts   Pueblo pottery
Mohawk masks   Haida blankets   Pomo baskets   Menominee copper
& the price of those things when whites sell them
to each other after buying them from us for dimes
or taking them
I like to remember some of our most beautiful creations
dying in german & british museums
I like to remember the darkness of our world
where our lives are mere inconveniences to their acquisition
I need to remember that the Native design towels
I want to buy at macy's   fill a white man's pocket
I like to think of our relationship
boiled to a simple phrase
They take   We give
They take more

in Honor of ELLEN KUZWAYO

MISS GLORIA IS

Black as Beautifull is Bold
strutting past midnight
with a flick of her eyelids
Could be dawn over there
toss of her shoulders
Dreads hanging down like somebody who knows
the ropes & in a pinch
could walk a circus highwire
over upturned faces & get 'em
clapping as she takes their sighs
away
Her feet purple or turquoise or red as she
dances what you'd better know
don't forget it now
'cause she could see
you   'cause she dangerously sweet
but no saint
'cause she beees
exactly what she be
leaves you
wanting some

for GLORIA JENNIFER JACKSON YAMATO

A SONG FOR MY PEOPLE

whose eyes I wear in my soul
in joyous praise of our gnarled hands
precious children   laughter in the soup of pain
Everyone of us beautifull
deeply as young pink birches in high white snowdrifts
the Native woman whose Black pimp stared me down
the many in the alcohol trap chewing off their legs
the strong, the fearful, the weary, the angry,
the traditional, the assimilated, the ones on both sides
of the bloody borders
playing bingo, dancing in Pow Wows
telling stories leaning against a cold fender
How beautifull we are   How complete
just as we are
Grief & confusion wail through our hills
Above it I sing a song for my people
who always resist   always fight
A song rising in our throats now
A song in our bellies now
A song in our hands now
A dark light in our eyes now
How we are beautifull

My Tears Are Wings
Chrysalos 1990

THIS IS WHERE I WAS BORN

but it's not mine
Tears as she tries to speak in english
not her first language
Can't remember the words of her roots
Decided to stop because people laughed
What does it mean when they chain up our tongues
When they take our languages
they take our lives
Not just language but everything
my family did
Couldn't talk about them in school
Everybody laughed
Her face a rupturing dam
Ashamed, I mocked my mother
So afterawhile
I just stopped talking

ON MY WAY

to washington, d.c. to speak for Lesbian rights
it all started when I agreed
to lecture 200 students at the university on anti-racism
I did well enough though I was at the bottom of a bowl of seats
with a few scattered notes & a weariness with the subject
deep enough to scream
There was the usual white guy saying he agreed
with everything I said
who couldn't go on when I asked him if he realized
how patronizing it sounded for him to say that
& the usual white gal on the verge of hysteria
who accused me of making him uncomfortable
& claimed that reverse racism is real
because twelve Black girls in her high school beat her up once
& the usual students of Color relieved to hear me
or anybody
then speaking eloquently of their own experiences
There was the usual applause   tears of those I had touched
Then a woman came up very close to me
I thought she was a Dyke & then she said,
I'm a white person as you can see,
WHY do they always think they have to tell us that?!
and when things go wrong it's always my fault.
I want to know why you people
WHY are we always you people?!
can't see that this is your fault.
She started to tell me that we didn't have
to live as we do & as usual   little bits of steam started
around my ears & then she said
Are you a Lesbian?
Yes   I said
You're sick!   she said with the usual venom
My arm went back fury sudden hot
& in front of the departing students I screamed
I am not sick! Get out of my face!
Oh she was happy then to see me being

the savage she knew I was
& how ashamed as usual I was that she could get me
in the throat   touch my last raw tired nerve & blow up
my heart   I hurried away   She chased after me
to tell me two more times at the top of her lungs
that I was sick
I shouted at her again in the halls my fists still clenched
Her age all that stopped me
Respect your elders   I hear my father murmur
She taunts me again   *You'll go to the penitentiary*
if you hit me
quite proud of herself
I shouted back   *That's the only reason I haven't!*
A Native student with tears in her eyes held me
Some Black women encouraged me
Some white women thanked me
I had a plane to catch
all the way to the airport   all the way to d.c.   all the time
I was in d.c. my heart raced I held in tears as well as I could
as usual
That old woman would tell you this grief & rage are all
my own fault   That she didn't ruin my elation
at going to d.c. with thousands and thousands
of other Lesbians   That it's my own fault I'm poor Queer
& unhappy with america   She'd tell you that just as she thought
I'm a savage & we're all sick
Will you shout it with me now
We're not sick
Again
We're not sick

especially for DONNA LANGSTON

IN THE BLACK STONE

mother looms flickering thin flame of light
her heavy breasts vague
I've held out my arms to her
brought them down in scars
Once   she sent me an envelope of wonderous autumn leaves
She knew I would love their brilliant colors
It was our finest moment
& singular
in our confused cries
I loved her   I was her mother when I was a child
cradling her against her mother's cold longing for a son
I hated her   when I found my looming need to be held
Nowhere to burn that old letter which flickers still
in these words
as autumn leaves fall over the circle of fire
our heavy hearts vague a long silence fields deep
where high winds blow confused
How can I
light myself steady
in this dark thin stone

YOU ASK FOR ARTIFICIAL TEARS

in this snarl we've caused which chokes us
Turns your head to the wall   I search store shelves carefully
Pick up apple juice   hot sauce   cat food   Finger the candybars
Wonder which of these could be tears   Where is
the place where my tears are dry & yours flow
I melt in coals you've learned to walk over
My arm knocks you off   I stumble apologies
We're similar in our stubbornness though you cling
with certainty to the cessation of pain
while I grasp it as my necessary heartbeat
You turn your back on me here or there
I don't show up as arranged
You tell me things I don't want to know
Pierce pain no one else sees
You assume I could let someone else see
& I cannot
Somewhere our languages are a drum we both understand
It seems my car is leaking oil   has no rear brakes
so any journey is dangerous
Hazard greater than this drum I need   as you need
while your car has been savaged by an incompetent mechanic
& rats who've chewed through the electrical system
You're not sure you can trust me to arrive at the drum   I hide
my grief with careful necessity
Hands empty
from the store   I give you dried lavender from my garden
weeps for us

ANTHROPOLOGY

We have been conducting an extensive footnoted annotated indexed & complicated study of the caucasian culture hereafter to be referred to as the cauks for ease in translation.

The most important religious ritual, one central to all groups, is the mixing of feces & urine with water. This rite occurs regularly on a daily basis & seems to be a cornerstone of the culture's belief system. The urns for this purpose are commonly porcelain, of various hues, although white is the most frequently used. The very wealthy rulers have receptacles of carved onyx or malachite with gold-plated fixtures. We have been unable to determine what prayers are said during this ritual because of its solitary nature & the fact that the door to the prayer room is always shut.

The main function of the majority of non-city dwellers is the production of an object called a lawn. Numerous tools for the cultivation of this lawn are sold in the marketplaces. It appears also to have a sacred character, as no activity occurs on it & keeping it short green & square is a constant activity.

The main diet of the culture is available from pushbutton machines or orange plastic small markets & was found by our researchers to be completely inedible. It is truly amazing what the human animal can subsist on.

Another prominent feature of the cauks is the construction of huge monuments built in clusters in the villages. These are not living quarters but are used about five days of the week for a ritual involving papers which appear to be sacred, given the life or death quality with which they are handled. The papers are passed about, often with consternation & eventually cast away when the spell is complete.

The mechanisms for healing disease appear to our eyes to be woefully complex & at the same time, inadequate. People who are seriously ill are quarantined in jails of pale green or white & often used to feed machines which appear to run on human blood.

Children who are born deformed in any way are usually confined to jails built for the purpose. The elderly are also jailed, there being no value system of respect for them. Those passing through transitions are called "crazy" & also jailed. Animals from distant lands again are jailed. In fact, there is some discussion of an alternative theory of central religious belief—that the actual spiritual purpose of the culture, is to jail as much as possible. Extensive use of fences is the key argument for this theory.

Our data is as yet incomplete. We hope by 1992 to have a more comprehensive overview, at which time a traveling exhibition of artifacts (including exhumed bodies to illustrate their burial practices) will tour for the education of all. Their attitude toward all non-cauk peoples is extremely hostile & violent. Many of our researchers have been massacred & yet, in the interests of science, we persevere.

for LOUISE BENALLY & her family

GATE #9

Driving across the border the guard was suspicious asked even more questions than usual   I was charming & stupid finally he let us through   Later we found out that Native people have blockades up all over canada to prevent whites from coming on the reservations in support of the situation at Oka & I understood   He thought our big boxes full of tent & sleeping bags were supplies for the blockade They would have been if we'd heard about it, but of course, we'd had no news in the states   Amanda says the situation is quite volatile with whites blockading towns to prevent Native access in retaliation —which isn't "new," simply more overt than usual   They're also hanging effigies of Native people & talking about moving in troops

    All over a stupid golf course, which honestly we don't need   A cop was shot, so of course the hysteria is high   500 dead Indians wouldn't even be cause for a hiccup   There are no other Indians waiting for this plane   Whites whites whites everywhere, they're a plague   Once Native people lived here   Now it's the death & noise of an airport & I'm using it

Earlier when I was reaching for a towel to dry my hands in the bathroom, a white "lady" cut in front of me & literally snatched the towel out of my hands to use it herself   When I looked at her, she said *Thank You* in that condescending way they have which silences any response & humiliates us   This is a little thing, the daily attrition we are supposed to endure numbly   We are called savage but there are no people more savage in their greed & arrogance than whites   None   Not just in some distant, shameful past but now   A white lesbian told me a few days ago that her grandmother *"hates Indians"*   She apparently has no sense of responsibility to "me" or to "us" to speak to her grandmother to bring about under-standing   I'm not sure why she told me this, we're not friends, I'd done a reading in a classroom, she was one of the students & I should know by now, that speaking out makes one a dumping ground for the toxic wastes of racism   I can't help hating HER for telling me some-thing I already know & spend my time constantly trying to repel Whites "hate us" because they've treated us inhumanely—savagely   Any of us who have survived are ugly reminders of their past & present viciousness   We are witnesses to the fact that these lands, all of them, town & reservation alike, *are our home*. No white person (or indeed, no non-Native person) has a "right" to be here When we survive (especially if we're sober & activists, as I am), we are "unpleasant" reminders of everyone else's invasion and / or genocide

There is an older man with white hair & cowboy boots, whose blonde, gum-chewing daughter sits bored beside him, who has been staring at me as I write this (*YES AMAZIN' FACTS OF NATURE* there are Indians who read & write)   I want to go up to him & say *Fuck you*   I'm "not allowed" in the prison of racism to notice his attempt at intimidation or to respond in any way   He's one of the guards of the system, a regulator   This is a familiar stare, one quite common, the "mildest" form of racism   Usually if you pretend "not to notice it," nothing escalates   We, People of Color, are stared at so much that we have high blood pressure, ulcers & alcoholism   It occurs to me, as I write this through the drivel of the stewardess rattling off the safety instructions (WHY don't they just have a tape recording?!), that all of us are profoundly reduced by racism—to surviving it, with very little resources left to overthrow it
     Of course, they also have superior fire power   We have managed to figure out that getting shot when you're brown is extraordinarily easy   Whether I cry, get angry or eat a chocolate bar (alcohol no longer being an option), in response to having a towel snatched from my hands (how could I be so petty to notice), I end up feeling like a hamster spinning my tinny wheel   Even though I know that is the exact intention   Racism is surrealism   Bizarre
     We are stuck with the trash no matter how we respond Whatever I was thinking before my privacy & dignity were violated, is lost forever   My spirit was ruptured   On the other hand, she didn't cut my throat   Because we are so often murdered, raped, imprisoned, tortured—or our families are—we numb ourselves to this petite bourgeoisie racism   I've even said in speeches that I usually escape the worst of racism   Compared to the actual facts, this is the truth   I'm still alive

Halfway to winnipeg, I'm trapped in the fruitless question of what

81

should I have done   Slapped her across the face?   Grabbed the towel back out of her hands?   Snatched her purse?   Stepped on her foot?   Vomited on her with a quick finger down my throat?

   Bit her on the neck & gotten blood on her new blouse?   All these possibilities delight me & ease the knot

I've been thinking lately of starting up a guerrilla warfare team against racism using sarcasm & dreaming up snappy comebacks *Excuse me but the charge for staring at me is $5 a second   You owe me $200 & we're going to small claims court if you don't pay up now*

   And writing a book entitled *One Day's Racist Incidents In A Three Square Mile Area*   It would probably run several volumes & even I'll admit has no commercial potential   Maybe the "american studies association" would publish it   Naw, I don't have a pedigree   We could certainly employ the homeless as door-to-door canvassers & solve several problems   We could start a chain letter of racist incidents!   We could have a grand prize for the worst story every week!   We could have slips of paper & draw a sample for scientific analysis!   We could have an anti-racism game show!   An anti-racism soap opera!   We could have educational films on airplanes!   We could have bingo games!   Let's get this going!   Workshops only reach the partially converted   We need a tent preacher!   We need a rock & roll band!   Free balloons for the children!   We need anti-racist bubble gum, cars, washing machines!   No more conferences   No more protest marches No more articles in papers only we read   Let's form an anti-racist corporation, a multi-national!   Think of the tax breaks!

At least, I've decided I'm going to start writing down every racist and anti-Jewish incident that happens to me, my family, my friends, my lovers, every one I hear about or see or smell or feel   Look for my 3,000-volume reference work coming soon   A major motion picture starring real people   No acting allowed   I can forget the stupid towel now   Let's all go back to what we were thinking about before

especially for MARLENE C. WONG & KAREN G. FREDRICKSON

NEAR YOUR BIRTHDAY

someones's old nest
has fallen into my fire
sweet smoky
Slowly the first snow melts in curves
white berries fatten
One of the nets
down at the salmon hatchery
has broken
raucous gulls call their delight
wings drifting in piles
Over there
where the sun will set
the mountains
dance forgiveness

for JANE

DON'T TRY

to kiss me into shape   I've the print of hundreds of lips
in every part of my body   Already heard about my long
luscious legs my silky thighs my impossibly smooth skin
my passionate hands   I've been an expert at sex
since he taught me how
Whatever it is that women who weren't abused give
I don't have it
I was torched out long ago   I respond as a knee jerks
to rubber hammer blows   I even enjoy myself
but it doesn't mean I'm giving you me
I don't have a self I can
give
Every piece of me that's still left
I need
I learned to fake being normal   to wear the camouflage
of whoever's in charge
Don't be deceived
I want to stay out of jail & the nut house & I'll do
whatever's necessary
You can't rely on me for anything
You certainly can't ask me to trust you
an oxymoron
Where would I have learned what trust means
Everybody has agreed to be fooled by my act for a long time
some of me is real some isn't
I don't know which is which
during the time I was supposed to be figuring it out
I was busy keeping my mother out of the bin for severe depression
taking care of my brothers & sister while servicing
& pleasing the man who is still
the longest relationship I've had
Don't assume that because I laugh so much I'm happy
mas que nada   better than nothing I survive
I can't talk to you about this because I don't know
what's real   what are my mother's feelings?   his?   what is
fear still thudding in my chest   I thought I loved him then

He told me I did
How can I explain chaos confusion so deep I don't know
when I want to
or when I do   because you want to
I know when you want to
before you even figure it out
I had to learn how to feel desire before it came at me so I could
escape
I'm not here now as I write
I've been pretending & lying for so long in order to be safe
What could I say to you that wouldn't be another lie
or wouldn't be true tomorrow
The only consistency in my life was violence & loneliness
I'm astounded to have friends who care about me
especially because I haven't always been a good friend
Too much intimacy & my blood begins to snap
Closeness means I can't say no
can't think means I'm not allowed to know or feel
means I'll be punished   You ask me what I want
assume I'm being smart when I don't know or say I don't care
Wanting was scorched out of me   Think of me as a burn victim
in constant pain who functions & endures   who thinks of
death as relief and friend
You don't survive my childhood
you dodge it

for my friend, MARTHA WALTERS

EVERYTHING IN ME

faces out to sea as she dreams I leave her
cries all night in her sleep while the water moves
moving laps the edges of our faces as we watch the sun
dip low in red dancing sashes swaying   leaving
We dream we are whole   Wake to find
ourselves scattered in other people's clothes
Packing ourselves out again
we cry like coyotes down in the canyon
echoing at the hawks which spin
up on the ridge where sun moves watery dreaming
that she laps the hands of another world
In the night cries we pack our lost loves
into the edges of our dreams
We wake remembering love
like red water lapping our faces
The coyote in my heart
is going somewhere else while my regrets wash to sea
I've packed myself in for the winter
I'll leave in spring swaying
at the red yarn of her arms weeping as I scatter
dreams that we are one

GOLDEN

kelp like autumn leaves rides
the slate satin sea
Sleepy swells billow voluptuously
Chiaroscuro waves lace over in jade exhilaration
mirroring the bellies of gulls
rosy in the falling sun

SOUVENIR OF WINNIPEG

They have him on trial to see
if he is sane enough to face charges
of 2 counts of attempted murder
2 counts of buggery
2 counts of unlawful confinement
2 counts of indecent assault
I assume the innocent fifteen-year-old girls who survived
are white
because this happens to the rest of us all the time &
nothing happens
He says the Black Angel has told him to kill himself

*   *   *

I am the Black Angel singing you to death
which comes too late   I am the Black Angel who avenges
all the women & children whose bodies are a constant
universal war zone for as long as we can remember
back into time
I demand you show me a woman who has not
been sexually wounded
who does not lie & manipulate & hate & please
in fear for her life or the lives of her children
who does not know any story of her mother or her sister
raped, beaten, humiliated, used, murdered
I have not met her
Forgiveness is the word in which we betray ourselves
and each other
I am the Black Angel who strips lies, cuts throats
severs the weapons of rapists
I am the sharp teeth of every woman mangled, tortured,
battered, bought & sold on the streets or the altar
I am the flame of kerosene brides burned alive in India
I am the sword of women selling their bodies & faces
in beauty pageants, singles clubs, modeling jobs,
graduate schools, country clubs & literary guilds

I am the Black Angel who will kill every man & boy on earth
who has ever abused a woman or child
knowing this will leave very few behind
I am the Black Angel whose wings are rage
whose robe is revenge   whose feet wear castration boots
whose hands are weapons
I am the Black Angel of our silence, our endurance
our bravery, our sobs, our eternal souls
which continue to love
Now it begins: A new Black Monday
Men jump from their towers in fear in thousands
in panic in millions
Women who have abused children, imitating men
leap to their deaths in shame
Now our Mother feeds my flight   brilliant red my eyes
I am the Black angel my heart beating your death
My fists clenching with your sins
My back a razor of the wreckage you've left
I am the Black Angel
I am dancing you to death
so we & our children may live in peace
I am the Black Angel whose voice knows no forgiveness
whose rage cannot be bought or appeased or denied
or destroyed
I am the Black Angel
Beware

GOING THROUGH

longview washington the death corset girdles the sky
in flashing white surreal smoke
which over us hovers changing into an angry gray bull elk
horns lowered to charge
These are the hills where bear hunted sweet berries
We women rubbed our hair with their grease
This was a song requiring many harmonies
a sky blue as a drum   flute sweet as spring
where we polished the word roam
until it shone
Over our obsidian hair
rosy-tailed hawks circle in slow light
This smoke winds dangerous bandages over our eyes
barbed wire tangles the air
We can no longer see the wild grasses
whose love flew into our baskets
Trees weep brown who have always been green
their songs hunger for bears
We're lonely   they cry
with no one to rub their backs on us
River turns in her sleep
Where are my sweet salmon?
Sky is gray with fear
Earth buckles sways under the wound of black roads
which don't breathe
Wild rose has left orphan roots who whisper
Where are the women who braided their hair in our sweet place
who wove our beauty on their moccasin toes?

We're hungry for a blue
that will sing like a drum
We're lifting our spring feet
to dance this death down
Having watched her
bend & change
when she meets angry stone
We grow
while she is gone   speaking of us in other skies
wild roses bloom
in her honor
from our eyes

in Honor of DIAN MILLION, inspired by the writing of ELIZABETH WOODY

I MAKE THE FIRE

as the sun rises   gold to gold
smoky britches in the sky
boogie down wood   snap & pop
Across my shoulder falls
shadow of Eagle
as I go to the wood shed
Tiny green feathers of new growth fir
curl & dance under my feet
Heavy winds last night
In my arms a sweet smell of cedar
debris from the shake mill
I'm a woman who carries kindling
& her past
as she prays

for CELESTE GEORGE

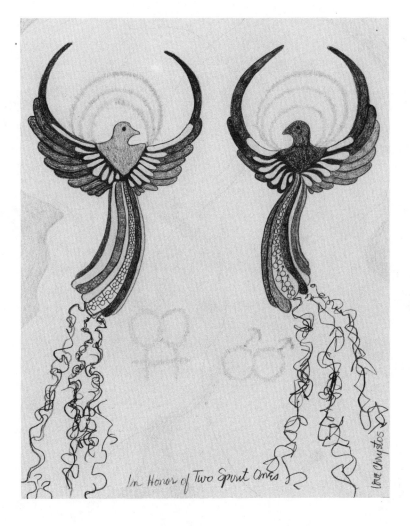

In Honor of Two Spirit Ones

Love Chrystos

DREAM LESBIAN LOVER

is there when I get home from work but allows me silence
to unravel or better yet   isn't there
but has left a note & a little surprise
She rubs my feet for hours
She wants to love me till I can't stand no more
& she rolls over to me so sweet
Dream lover cooks me hot meals & washes up after
Never arrives without flowers & only brings my favorites
Dream lover has long fingers   a patient playful tongue
& thrives on five hours sleep a night
She could play the harmonica   weave pine needle baskets
bead me a wedding sash   write me lust poems & love poems
Dream lover has eyes deep as the sky   feels herself in others
feels our connecting bones   Rises early in the morning
to make the best rich coffee
Aah she could bring you to your knees with a look
& does
Dreamy woman has a bed of lace & roses & home
She could build a fire in the rain
Could always fix my car for free
Could call the dentist to make my appointment
Iron my shirt when I'm in a hurry
Knows how to make chocolate mousse   chocolate silk pie
black bottom cupcakes   molasses cookies   sour cream cake
lemon pound cake & fresh mango ice cream
O such a creamy dreamy one
She's showing up tonight with a butch pout & a femme slink
a tough stance & a long knowing
Dream lover
she won't have any other girlfriends
but won't mind
if I do

a *Personals Ad*, with tongue in cheek

SONG FOR A DOE

MOTHER VOICE:
> I will die with your broken skewed leg
> stiff body beside the road
> in my heart carried for years under
> layers of grief thick as blood

GRANDMOTHER VOICE:
> We saw you
> twice on subjugation day
> once as we drove
> through a sky of lingering apricot gauze
> still
> wide-eyed, alive   Too close to the road
> as we went up to the Rez to watch the fireworks stands
> have a giveaway showdown for hours outdoing
> one another in flowers of colored flames
> Again, exhausted from explosions & overexcited crowds
> as we came home
> Your eyes a glitter in the dark
> too close to the road
> We prayed for your safety

CHILD VOICE:
> This morning I went over to get the mail
> & while waiting in the post office, bored
> I stamped my hand in crimson
> *Perishable*

MOTHER VOICE:
> Distracted in the whirlwind of my mind I saw you
> this time   Too close to the road
> an explosion of bent back ear   torn filmy eyes   scraped hide   flies
> I stopped my car
> went to you weeping weeping stroking your hard fur
> your soft cool hooves

My tears raising tiny clouds of dust as they splashed you
Weeping I sit beside you for a long time touching your death
A white woman jogs by
Oh Dear Oh Dear   she says
keeps going
I don't know
if your death or my tears for it
was what frightened her
I am unseemly in a public place
No one sits grieving by a damn deer hit by a car
I weep now

GRANDMOTHER VOICE:
The road crew will probably come today & take you
to the dumps
Whoever hit you
didn't know
they owed it to you
to eat you or pass you on
Some people would call you a road pancake
Almost nobody would weep for you
which is why
I have to weep so hard

MOTHER VOICE:
You were a first year mother
your swollen nipples stiff & erect in death
Were you searching for your fawn
who maybe was hit yesterday & cleared away as debris
or is your fawn still alive
& hungry

GRANDMOTHER VOICE:
They were probably drinking it was a holiday
certainly driving much too fast on this winding road
I hate them
I sit beside you hating people hating cars hating
with the clear wound of a child

DRUM VOICE:

You catch in my mind a barb I cannot pull free
without unraveling myself

MOTHER VOICE:

I smudge myself   burn Sweet Grass   I weep
I'm sitting with you beside this road
until I am an old old woman
My eyes on fire with the life I saw in yours until

GRANDMOTHER VOICE:

Once home I stroke & stroke my old cat until she's silk
her purring holds my tears
her life, her fur brings me back
I'll be expected to smile tonight   make small talk
it's the way our grief is killed
until we have to drink or drug or hurt ourselves to feel it
as crazy, we act as though we're normal
& this hollow place
is what we'll accept
I cannot bring you back

MOTHER VOICE:

Your life was absolutely necessary
to mine
Your eyes wild & open
are the water I must have
in this concrete desert that they want to name reality

GRANDMOTHER VOICE:

All
that land around there is cut up for sale
pretty soon there won't be any place for you
Nothing but ostentatious houses
Everybody will drive fast on this road
kill whatever's left after the bulldozers are done killing
None of them will remember you

DRUM VOICE:

I am the woman whose heart is a deer
broken & skewed
My eyes filmy
I grow old with grief
surrounded by insipid laughter
idle chatter
most of the children
already unable to weep
buried alive in artificial happiness
starving to death inside things & things & things

MOTHER VOICE:

My body tears the thud of death echoes in my hands

CHILD VOICE:

Young mother I am weeping my face stiff with salt
I grieve alone
The word on the back of my hand
has blurred to a red stain like blood

for ELANA MYERSON & ELIZABETH MARKELL
July 5, 1990   Bainbridge Island

(there are many forms of genocide and this is one)

SHAME ON!

fake shamen give me some money
I'll make you a catholic priest in a week
couple thousand I'll name you pope
of our crystal breakfast cereal circle of healers
Give me some money   you'll be free
Give me some money   you'll be whole
Give me some money   you'll be right
with past lives zooming by your door
Steal from anybody to make a paste-up tacked-on
holy cat box of nothing
I tell you I'm sincere & that excuses everything
I'm a sincere thief   a sincere rapist   a sincere killer
My heart is pure my head is fuzzy give me some money
& you'll be clear
Your pockets will be anyhow
Give me a dime   I'll ease your crime
Give me a dollar give me a ten give me a thousand
fastest growing business in america
is shame men   shame women
You could have a sweat same as you took manhatten
you could initiate people same as into the elks
with a bit of light around your head
& some "Indian" jewelry from hong kong why you're all set
Come on now take something more that doesn't belong to you
Come on & take that's what you know best
White takes   Red turns away
Listen I've got a whole bunch of holey underpants
you could use in a ceremony you can make up yourself
Be a born again Indian it's easy
You want to buy spiritual enlightenment we got plenty
& if you act today we'll throw in four free 100-watt lightbulbs
so you can have your own private halo
What did you say? You met lynn andrews in person?
That woman ought to be in a bitter herb stew

I'll sell you lies half-price better than hers
america is starving to death for spiritual meaning
It's the price you pay for taking everything
It's the price you pay for buying everything
It's the price you pay for loving your stuff more than life
Everything goes on without you
You can't hear the grass breathe
because you're too busy talking
about being an Indian holy woman two hundred years ago
You sure must stink if you didn't let go
The wind doesn't want to talk to you
because you're always right
even when you don't know what you're talking about
We've been polite for five hundred years
& you still don't get it
Take nothing you cannot return
Give to others   give more
Walk quietly   Do what needs to be done
Give thanks for your life
Respect all beings
simple
& it doesn't cost a penny

in Honor of MURIEL MIGUEL & SPIDERWOMAN THEATRE

THAT BLUE ENVELOPE

you took out of the garbage
demanded
to know who was writing me letters at my post office box
while I was on an important long distance call
Lost my voice thoughts stunned by your electric eyes
That blue envelope contained junk mail
about some kind of makeup
They handwrote the address
to fool me into opening it
Every box got one
Away from you I dream of that envelope
which spills open your rage possessive frightened
controlling brew across my pillow
Doesn't belong to me
What you're looking for is not in the garbage
or me
or in that blue envelope
You've made a box between us with your accusations
later denied
I'm guessing this isn't love
it's some other enemy junk from the garbage
something so
bloody blue

WE CUT OFF OUR HAIR

as our children kill themselves at fourteen or seventeen
in mass explosions
one after another until ten or twenty-three
are dead
on one reservation after another
multiplied across our land
Breathing this colonized air they take poison
into their hearts listening for the message
of genocide so much easier when we do it to ourselves
& save whites the trouble
Grief cuts out our hearts & laughs
din of this cruel survival breath to breath
going on through this pain we know strips us
crushes us beneath bulldozers & booze
We pray for you our children
LIVE
Become the river of our continuing hoop
LIVE
Become the breath of our never silent drums
LIVE
Become our future red & remembered
LIVE
Become our voices singing up the sun
LIVE

for ANNETTE JAIMES & WARD CHURCHILL

THE WOMEN WHO LOVE ME

have loud voices   laughter   interrupt excitedly
hold me with their breasts   cunts   hands   kiss my neck   bite
my shoulder   talk to me for hours about writing   hummingbirds
wild honeysuckle   trick towels   bleach & laundry
The Women Who Love Me enjoy my new shoes   share
spandex leggings & say I dress like the brimming full silver moon
whisper *LOOK OUT* in my ear when dangerous girls hover
Watch my back   my front
put their tongues down my throat   lick my ass
Let my fist bring the sun up in their pussies
We gossip   we cook   we wash up   we tell outrageous lies
The Women Who Love Me know how to write   fuck   paint   kiss
dance   hate & love
how to leave a woman & how to stay
The Women Who Love Me are usually resented by everybody else
nagged by disrespect or envy
& those who don't get enough sex
without realizing that none of us does either
or prefer books
They're the Lesbians mothers don't want to meet
who make shy girls blush from their feet up
They're out here on the same razor I walk shouting
the goddamn emperor is naked & so is the empress
& no   we won't be quiet
& yes we'll wake the neighbors & scare the postman
with our loud roars of delight
or *Honey where did you get those red lace gloves?!*
or that pin which says
Receive God / Bend Over
or *GIRL did you see the look that white woman gave you*
she's practicing her noose knots you'd better look out

Yes indeedy we're the Lesbians who receive all the shocked
appalled stares   clucking tongues   venomous spite
from everyone including our own
The Women Who Love Me are the women I adore
Just remember when you open your mouths to trash us
we're the ones carving out the tunnels
so you'll have room to breathe

for DOROTHY ALLISON & ALIX LAYMAN

I JUST PICKED THE FIRST RIPE

tomato from my garden cherishing her sensual cleft
gold freckles around stiff hairy sepals
Inhaling deeply her sharp smell   my nose pressed
to smooth bursting flesh   Kissing pure skin
planning to eat her like a peach
juice dripping down my neck
very slowly
because it's september after a rainy cool summer
The rest of the vine may stay green
have to be brought inside   carefully wrapped in paper
to eventually turn orange but not red hot
glowing with sun
as this
who could be
the only one

especially for JANICE GOULD & MIMI WHEATWIND

EXCUSE ME MA'AM

can I give you a dollar?
I said to the old woman leaning with her bags
against the marble façade of the brooks brothers building
with a slaughtered lamb hanging over us
Not enough but all I had on this cold morning
on my way across town to a maid job
She shook her head wouldn't look up at me
I ran for the bus which didn't wait   All day
as I scrubbed I wondered what would be enough
Excuse me Ma'am can I give you a 100 dollars   a red rose
a new coat   warm mittens   a good meal   a greyhound ticket
Excuse me Ma'am
can I give you a home?

FOR YEARS

I've kept every scrap of paper, old letters, expired coupons, ticket stubs, grocery lists, ideas for how to improve my life or apartment, 47 copies of the same embarrassing poem I'll never publish because it's trite or sentimental, some piece that I might be able to use in some project of a paperless future. It's partly the result of seeing clear cuts. Partly my fragile sense of self, direct result of living in a country that has made me invisible. I am clinging, proving my existence. Somebody loved me sometime somewhere or at least tried to. Or said they did. I want the whole world to love me. Applause is an addiction, like any other. It embarrasses & frightens me, I turn away, but could I stand it if an audience shrugged & left?

Yesterday I decided I was a fool to show my soul on stage. It's hypocrisy, idiocy, the worst trick of colonizer culture. *Hey man show us your guts that's a gorgeous shade of red!* I'm feeding that terrible craving to be amused, startled, toyed with. Poets are slow motion Mad Max movies. *LOOK* we shout, at this gore & this abomination & this thrill & then this. I can't afford special effects. Making poems is walking into the firing range. Between the cross lines are all the minor & major lies that writing tells. It reassures us that experience can be jelled in words. That we will be defended, safe, remembered.

That loss is not loss if we write about it. You may be gone but I have these words I strung together like beadwork & you, yourself have been captured.

Traps. We want more & more traps. We want to keep everything. Some of the environmentalists want to keep the scenery, some of the animals but no people. At least, none except for themselves on sunday hikes.

Tell each other always, forever, no other. Build our private moats, drawbridges, corrals. You be my dog, wife, husband, lover, child, car, house, clock, vcr. Let me think I can own you so I don't have to face my death which I don't own, don't know, which is the terrible stranger we project onto others. You look like my death so I'm going to hate you. You look like you might know more about my death than I do & I hate you even more. We hate our jobs. Some hate our children. We hate having to get up from the couch to get a glass of water. Buy me a robot that will die for me, I can handle the drinks & dishes & broom.

Buy me red shoes which will make me forget the dreariness of my jobs, rent, bills, the loneliness that crowds in at the windows leaving a gray smudge we think we scrub off in hot showers in the morning getting ready for a new day, our dreams stuffed in the closet bent & mildewing. I don't like my Lesbian neighbors. My tribe is thousands of miles away. My family in scattered bouquets fights to keep a sliver of the american dream up their asses. It's that or die. It's that or stay drunk until we die.

How can we live with strangers, eat with strangers, travel with strangers, work with strangers, sell our souls to strangers, watch strangers on tv, buy food with strangers? It makes us stranger & stranger until we can't remember the names we came here with. Until we can't remember what color the sky is. Knee jerk say, *It's blue.* Until the moon becomes some place to leave your used toilet paper & golf clubs. Until we are all buying & selling things we don't even touch. Here we are in the worst possible mess. Praying to Spirits who have probably got fed up with us & gone fishing in another universe. It's up to us now. We have to get ourselves out of this jam, this jelly, this junk. No one is gonna save us. We don't need fluoride in our water, we need compassion.

This morning as the sun dappled my studio window through rain dripping from the roof, I forgave myself these cascading papers which pile on the floor & sofas, these unanswered letters. I've joked that I'm practicing to become a bad lady. I meant to write bag lady but it's so good I have to leave it in. I know why they keep what others call garbage. To prove that, they too, exist. See, here's all their stuff in your way at the bus stop, where they've spent the night. They don't have anything else to acquire. The human need to own something is powerful. They protect themselves from robbery on these dangerous streets by owning bags no one wants, no one could sell later for a few dollars. I thought of buying the bags from the ladies & installing them in a chic modern art gallery. The ladies probably wouldn't sell their bags—too personal. The bags *would* sell in the galleries, for thousands of dollars, collectors being the weird people they are. We could open a homeless shelter with the money. That's what I'm doing when I win the lottery. I'm serious.

I think of bundles, of the necessity for mystery, a place wrapped, a place that only one person opens. I think of courage, the freedom & risk to live outside of old age prisons. Think of the dawn & air & birds, which no one owns. Think of all the life a bag lady carries in her weary arms. Think of poverty, hunger, war, those mainstays of government. Pieces of paper prove we're alive. Birth certificate. Checkbook. Insurance premium. Mortgage. Lease. Driver's license.

You can be arrested for not having any identification. The jails are so overcrowded that they rarely bother anymore. Still a law. Vagrancy. The crime of having nothing & no place to go.

FROM THE OTHER WORLD

the dead call to me singing in voices I barely remember
memory such a fickle lover
their passage has left me dry
Carrying the weight of too many coffins
braced for more to come
I am a young woman still
learning how alcohol   plagues   bad luck   bad driving
can strip me of the light in eyes I need
My heart fills with fog   old tears blow across my face
sometimes I feel I should just give up
wear nothing but black
whose calm darkness will comfort & hide my sorrow
In the other world they dream of my words
send them for me in the wind
I hear crying low over the water that is our loss
We are a people for whom death is common as colds
we stagger under grief not even able
to lean on one another because no one stays rooted
in a hurricane
Rain comes from the south blowing hard
the grass lies down until it is over
We hardly speak of the deaths for we know
we have years more to carry
The hatred we have had to withstand storms on
There is little pity for us in the hearts
we live among
as we face time
with no shelter

for VALERIE STREET

VAMPIRE

She came spewing hearts & forever & I need you in my sheets
promising begging charming she'd give anything
if only I'd stay
Sounded like some dream come true
What she meant was give me   pay attention to me   love only me
Anything she gave a rope tightening
Everything she did for me a steel-spring trap
crushing my legs until I spit gasping   *Anything*
I'll do anything
if you'll go away & leave me alone for three hours
Every boundary I drew washed under tears accusations
cruel remarks on my flaws
which I knew by heart & in detail before we were through
Every friend who wanted an evening with me a battleground
My every late arrival equaled a secret rendezvous
I answered questions concerning my whereabouts
from 12:15 p.m. to 1:38 p.m.
My letters read   My journals invaded so often
I stopped keeping them   then started locking them in my car
I ended ready to sell my dearest books
for silence & privacy
Drained I wondered why love was so difficult
She's so delightful   I love her
You'd all like her instantly   What was wrong with me
Maimed unable to trust I hated others   afraid of yet another
scene at someone's dinner party or back porch
or guest bedroom
Now it's over two years later still nagged with guilt
because she loved
me I'll give anything
to never see or hear her again

IT WAS A SATURDAY

I was spending the weekend with them, probably to babysit that night, my mother often arranged these visits   Her sister had six children, they needed help, I was my mother's oldest   He was like a father to me, they said he spoiled me, really   He'd convinced me I was in love with him, so my reluctance was hidden even from myself

We went out to work at one of his mansions in the old green truck, where sometimes I'd jack him off or suck his dick in the parking lot down at the old sutro's baths   It was still an ice skating rink then, before it burned down the last time   His clients were in europe, he was caretaking, it must have been late summer, don't remember how old I was   Maybe thirteen   It had been going on for awhile, I didn't think I had a choice   Like cooking dinners & cleaning house

He turned on the sprinkler system & then took me down in the basement   Years before it had been the servants' quarters   The old iron bedsteads & mattresses & dressers were still there   No sheets or blankets   But trinkets & faded things left behind   Dull lavender silk violets in a mashed bunch on a chair   Cobwebs   A gray ribbon that had once been pink on the floor   I was wandering in the different rooms, imagining what it must have been like to live with one tiny barred window to the sun, underneath the ground & the people one served for probably fourteen hours a day   Was this the cook's room or the upstairs maid's?   How old were they when they went into service?   What happened to them?   Are their children alive?   Does anyone remember these rooms?   The people upstairs are so rich that they allow them to decay   They don't need this space for anything, all the help lives outside now, no one is sheltered here   I wanted to cry down there, even before what happened next   He wanted to fuck again   That was what he usually wanted   It was always there under the friendly words or smiles or hot apple pie treat at zim's   I didn't like him fucking me, it hurt   Terribly   He could make me come with his tongue or his finger but never with his dick   I turned into a rag doll when he fucked me   Numb   My arms are still asleep

It was what he wanted to do, you go along with adults or they beat you   *That's the way life is, isn't it?*   So we started to fuck   I don't think we took off our clothes, it was cold down there & we couldn't stay long because he had other lawns to water   I was helping him   At the end of the day, he would give me five dollars   I was so proud of that money   It helped out at home & bought my school paper

Somehow he realized that I had fucked some high school boys since the last time he'd been at it   I was bigger inside or something Now I wonder if he could really have known   He yelled at me *Did you do it with somebody else?*   I can't remember if I lied or told the truth   He hit me   Black eye   Yelling & more yelling about how I had betrayed him   I was a whore & couldn't be trusted   Did I cry?   I cry sometimes to make people leave me alone   Or did I just stand there & take it, as I also do, thinking it will be over faster if I just let them rip   He left in a fury   I was afraid he was deserting me   I didn't know how to get home from there   It was the rich part of town with no buses, they'd call the cops if they saw me wandering around by myself   He was probably only clipping the bushes or raking the ground or something to make it look good to anyone who might be watching   Wanted to kill myself   Saw a rusty razor blade on the dresser   Tried to cut my wrists, sawed away unsuccessfully, although there were beads of blood, it was too dull   I didn't understand that it doesn't work, even with a sharp razor, you have to cut higher up where you can get an artery   That's the first time I tried to kill myself   I got better at it as I got older but didn't succeed   I still think about it as a solution to being in pain or numb   I write to thaw myself

He came back   More yelling   I was a no good useless cunt & a stupid fool   What did I want to go do that to myself for?   I didn't have the sense mon dieu gave me   More hitting   Threw my clothes at me so I must have been naked by then   He liked to look at my breasts *Get dressed, you can do that right can't you?* This is the man who really loves me, look at all he goes through for me, I believe him   Not that different from my mother when she screams at me hits me & says she loves me   Old dad too   *Isn't*

love being hurt until you can't take it anymore?   Maybe I was
crying by then because he shouted   *SHUT UP*   & I froze inside
Still frozen in that moment   *Is he going to kill me 'cause he's sick of
me?*   I can replay it   go back to the dim light of that room, dust,
shiny corroding mirror losing its silver on the back, ticking striped
mattress with buttons   whose prints were still in my back   I can
feel the scratch on my arm which would later be attributed to rose
thorns & my clumsiness   Glad my mother never paid attention to
me because she wouldn't notice the black eye   Worried my aunt
would   *I'm only supposed to fuck one person, the one who owns
me   But to feel alive & free, I have to fuck others, then it feels like
I'm choosing to fuck instead of having to*

My heart is racing as I write this   He'll show up on this porch,
hundreds of miles away, to shout that he loves me, I can't write this,
that I love him too   I'm betraying him   My most terrifying fear
is that I do love him   I was such a child I didn't know what to do
next   I obeyed   put on my clothes, went out & got in the truck
We went to the next mansion   I pulled weeds out of the lobelia
border   He cut back a wisteria vine   I never said a word to
anyone, not even him   I had learned so long ago that talking back
meant being hit

I'm going back in time & cut his dick off with the rusty razor   It
will take a long time & I'll thaw out while I'm doing it   Then I'll
bash his head in & leave quietly by the basement door he's left
ajar   I'll walk home   Home isn't safe so maybe I'll just walk out
to the beach & sit until something happens   If he comes here
tonight, I don't have to worry   I'll stab him & burn him piece by
piece in the wood stove   Nobody will ever know   Nothing's too
good for him

for Nuzzler, also called Uppi, Lloyd Smith's dog out at La Push

IMPACT

Crows spiral up suddenly   startling
me with a racket that can only mean Eagle
is skimming the meadow brush   hungry
cruising the rocky shore where Gulls & Pipers scour
for Mussels   Crabs   Oysters
Yesterday two young white men came to my door asking if
I saw Eagles
I wanted to know why   before I'd say
An environmental statement to prevent
the convention center from going in down the road
which I don't want either so I said   *Yes*
I've seen as many as three pairs circling together
but only 15 or 20 sightings over the last five years
because I usually have to work somewhere else during the day
He asked if I was a birdwatcher   I laughed
I can't afford binoculars & birds
are not separate beings I watch
I tried to tell him about the leaves
down there when the owner torched the old building
for the insurance & how just the day before
I thought I should dig up some of those old Native Rhodies
put them in my garden
because the lime leaking from the cement foundations
was turning their leaves brown
The Leaves   I said   *I saw the Leaves burn*
Deer come shocked running down the road
Later they broke the yellow tapes
warning of asbestos pollution
with their delicate legs
He didn't care about the Leaves
or the stink thick in our air for weeks after
It's a little late   I mumbled   *Deer don't read english*
I think an environmental statement on america is
probably too late
They were so anxious to know where the Eagles nested
I was vague

not ever rude enough to go looking for the home
of a being whose privacy is sacred
I pointed in the general direction
of a steep hillside where I know they don't nest
full of Madrona   Alder   Fir   Cedar
which is too sharp to log or build on
so will probably not need an environmental statement to keep
it that way
I wish I could give you the moment when
Eagle came back into view trailing Crows with the sun dancing
on the water near the very still meadow then you'd know
even one more building anywhere in america or the world
is too many

especially for VIV HASKELL

SHE HAS A PAIN IN HER NECK

I have a pain in my back   both of us incapacitated
with drugs to kill
the pain which don't
special pillows, braces, exercises, advice from everyone
to relax or try dr. X or naturopath Z or special arnica
lotion or meditation or lying flat in beds staring
at ceilings or lowering ourselves in hot baths or ice packs
It's the work we do I say
She laughs & agrees to be at another anti-racism
workshop in portland if they can fly her down
because sitting in a car or bus or train for three hours will
put her neck out
I schedule myself to arrive one day early at every
anti-racism conference, gathering, symposium, celebration
because I have to lie flat for a night before
or I'll be in too much pain to speak after traveling
three hours or six or nine to wherever
Do you know
how much we'd like to slap silly all the white women
we know who ride their bikes lift weights jog go for hikes
see Lesbian comedy & watered down music whose main
preoccupation is the care & feeding of their slender
"fit" bodies with complete apathy to the struggles
of anyone but themselves
& their clique of friends who, if they're lucky, one
happens to be Black or Asian or Chicano or Native & then
they get to be not racist
or whose sole political activity is going to meetings
with other whites about central america or africa
or going to see Sweet Honey in the Rock & feeling uplifted
& connected to oppression for weeks afterward?

It's the work we do I say
We nod & agree to participate in a workshop on power if
we can have a group for Women of Color only
to discuss internalized oppression
& ways to establish self-esteem in the teeth of racism
which is so poorly advertised that fewer than ten women come
& we are interrupted by three different white people &
one Asian woman in two hours time
claiming
we aren't supposed to be there / we aren't scheduled
we aren't on the agenda
as we point to our names on the program
where are our papers
they'll have to check with the office
if we can be there at all
And we laugh & we continue & we hope
that the women who came will be empowered healed encouraged
When my friends ask me how my back is   I shrug
usually say fine unless the pain is so bad
I can't keep the tears down
I know my one pitiful little lance is up against
a hydra that won't quit
& I'm a fool for trying
but I keep on / burned out / furious / insulted
demeaned / assaulted / ridiculed knowing this pain won't stop
until our work is done

for GLORIA JENNIFER JACKSON YAMATO

IDYLL: FOUR DAYS

We laughed so hard when we arrived at the tackiest motel room in the universe, replete with formica / chrome table & two rickety chairs, fake wood paneling & a spectacular view of the parking lot. In the coffin-sized bathroom, only one person could barely turn around. If you used the toilet, your knees were in the shower. If you bent to brush your teeth, your butt was in it. The kitchenette was of similar magnificent design. I needed to lose at least 35 pounds to fit in the narrow slot between the stove & sink—so I usually cooked & she washed up. I restrained myself from taking the marvelous sign on the back of the door: *DO NOT cook crabs in this room as it takes days to get the smell out.*

However, as you'll see, the setting faded very quickly into the closeup of new lust/tentative love, where each curve is all that one sees & nothing is as good as the taste of her cunt rippling.

There was a color tv, newer than anything else by 20 years, which we attempted to use as camouflage for our sounds. Not successfully, for the following afternoon, we got dirty looks from the crabby young husband next door. I was afraid we'd be thrown out because we're both so loud when we come. I'd forgotten that no one wants to admit publicly what great sex we can have—they can't complain without severely jeopardizing the myth that *We're only lesbians because we can't get a man.* Given how much everybody hates us—churches, governments, parents, schools, jobs, pizza takeouts, gas stations, banks—all the hate we have to shove off our backs everyday, we deserve hot sex. What a relief it is to be with a woman who is louder than I am, to never wonder did she come yet, or still, that awful quivering silence. I love to hear yes, uh huh, harder, deeper, slower & finally cries from the shaking belly I recognize as they rush through my blood on out the top of my head.

Our dear tacky motel was located on the oregon coast near oceanside, which is worth the seven hour drive from my place (also on a beach but one that is ringed like Malibu with houses, houses). You can walk for miles without hitting the barbed wire of Private Snobperty. The sand was full of amazing swirling patterns from the oil spills, which were quite beautiful, though I'd give them up for clean beaches. On the way down, broom blazed yellow beside the roads, with pale green rosebuds on the tips of all the evergreens. We drove under Blue Herons, Hawks, Eagles, an Osprey & some dark Geese very high up going north.

We met three months ago at a planning meeting for a National Lesbian Conference where we spoke intensely about politics. I don't remember a word now, as we glide through each other going to marches, speaking out, seeing political theatre which sounds like one of those earnest, sincere relationships with very little sex but I've never had sex so good. Just good. Sex where you spend all day in bed & never want to go back to work or talk to anyone else or put your clothes on. Sex that breathes. Sex that makes us wet in memory at roadside diners. She blushes when I talk about her pussy but she likes it. I know perfectly well that *Pussy* is not feminist but *I love your vagina* just doesn't have the right ring. Pussy has sibilance like sex when you finally get enough or you could get enough if you didn't have to sleep, after 25 years of trying. A few times getting enough but with other incompatibilities that soon soured into go away.

Have I finally figured out what I want with a woman & do I finally like myself enough to make sure I have it? We haven't fought since we met, we both consider this very odd, as veterans of long & short relationships in which we were always doing at least three things wrong & usually more; veterans of women who found our character flaws completely unacceptable but still wanted to go to bed with us, most likely so they could continue to tell us how angry they were about *x* or *t*. We joked throughout the trip about what we'd fight about without ever managing to get angry about anything. I'm accustomed to having a nasty battle about one week or two into my 4 or 5 or 8 year liaisons. It is important that we're both sober. She's accustomed to girlfriends who don't think she's emotional enough or she's too emotional or wants to spend too much time together or needs too much distance. I make her laugh, which is good, as she's very serious. She actually enjoys & appreciates me which is balm after years of fear, resentment, envy, anger. She is supposed to be looking for a job, I'm supposed to be writing a play and a novel. Instead we drove down to spend days in inner & outer seas. I brought sexy nightgowns I never unpacked. We were in bed so much I didn't have to bring any clothes at all. We planned every night to get dressed to go out for a fancy romantic dinner at the place just two doors away but we never made it. She bought dessert there one night & brought it back to our bed full of crumbs & wet spots. Once we limped in around noon for breakfast, neglecting to take showers so that throughout the meal we chuckled as we lifted forks to mouths, smelling ourselves.

She is plump, round, with nipples who adore being sucked. She is dark-eyed searing eyes in which I am calmed & held still. She is dark-haired with silver spider's silk weaving her years, dark hairs on her belly swirling down, her divine greed. I reel in her smell, wind, seaweed, her gentleness, her butchness, the way she leans over me, her arms are walls that shut out the noisy messy world & convince me that flesh sweet on flesh is all I care about. Her voice is deep, dark as she says hard words, shivery words, cunt squeezing words, hungry words, tasting me taste her.

Her mouth came looking for me   nibbling my nape, her belly pressed into my ass as I turned the pancakes smiling. The next batch burned. My hand on her ass playing with her crack as she grunts, my tongue looking around for that magenta spot who goes ahhh whhoooo uh huh

Her thighs slapping my ears, I reach to catch her head falling off the edge. I'm wet to my knees taking her until I'm mindless need. She thinks she wants to stop   *No baby*   I say   *Give me a little more I can feel it in you* & she does shouting over the feeble Motown tape

I smell my hands now when she has just left breathing in the light I've touched   Pulling her back into me pushing into her my heart swirling   My eyes weaving our names   Her skin that rises to meet me instead of drawing away & the restless hours before I'll have her in my hands again   pulling off her shirt   my teeth along her neck little bites   my tongue in her ear as she shudders half pulls away because it feels too good

& the restless hours before I have her in my arms again pulling
hours & hours 21 long hours before my fingers are warm inside her
where all the colors of life dance where she grips me so tightly my
hands cramp I don't care & go on reaching into her pushing to our
screams of joy wet glimmer of her lips tender rivulets roaring

In the evenings we went for walks when the tide was out, our eyes
intently searching for agates, of which we found many.

for ILENE SAMOWITZ

DEERHEART WHEREVER YOU ARE

Don't you know
by now that I've stopped answering my phone until I know
who it is   Everytime you hang up without a message I know
it's you   Everyone else is thrilled I got the machine you know
so I could avoid your wrenching accusing calls which you know
left me despairing for days even though I know
that's not what you meant to do   I know
you've been bragging you made love to her
on our living room floor as I slept in our bed you know that was tacky
I couldn't live with you anymore   said so   I know
she was your last thrust
blonde young college-educated rich slim pretty
all those wounds of mine I know
too well & shared with you until you know
how to flay me with your tongue as you loved me with it   Know
I loved you as far as I could go   I know
you know
Can't forget as you hold her   lying in her arms you say
I threw you out you know
why
four years of hell & paradise in your hands reflects in my mirror
as I feel anew intolerable scenes   threats   blocking my car
There was no excuse & I know
You didn't know
any other way   I know I won't get over you under you
around you away from you know
the love we made still pulses through
though the us we made is gone
Light falling on my hands this morning comforts me as I stare
at the phone I know you rang so recently   Minutes loop
like noose ropes   You're too sly to leave a vicious or loving
message that I know you wouldn't want me to play to anyone
as proof of what we both know
but you deny
According to the abuse handbook you did everything
but hit me I know

you didn't
so you could say you didn't abuse me   No bruise for proof
The wound of your insults far slower to heal I know
I believed that if I loved you long & hard enough you'd feel
it & know
we could live without your distorted rage which only I saw
I know you disagree have plenty of reasons to call it all
my fault   I know I betrayed you when I wouldn't be possessed
furious with me you know
I'm right   We had to separate   I wanted to do it without
this echo of taped dial tones   you taking my tools money
dictionaries   trashing me to our friends
I know
the thrust of how I saw us without illusion went too deep
We know we disagree   don't speak   I don't know
where you are   You know
I've changed the locks & hate me for it   Final sign that we
know I won't love you enough to let you charm me back
at my expense   You know
I'm avoiding the humiliation of sharing any more of my tears
with you I know this machine is stupid an illusion
of protection as we know

RE*ENTRY

With these words I'm gasping out of disintegration
sex is a prison of hatred   sex is a kingdom of death
between my legs is where all the trouble started
Do you think the leaves love me?
Hanging on to these words for breath
ladder away   rope out of   precious seeds of survival
Swimming against the current of my whole life rocks
betrayals   rotten relationships   violence   drugs   drink
These words are tiny
raindrops which will bring me to flower again
I've dressed my loneliness grief rage in words
as though they could keep me warm   keep out the rapists
prowling every street I walk
I have never been safe for longer than an hour
As though words could bring back the child
I was   before he wiped my mouth in shame   before he spit
into my body his fear   before he took my mind
and made it his
Until thirty years later this summer I still obey him
with my lovers   still bend myself concubine to their will
& do not know
what love is
Brainwashed to accept the dregs vile words lies
expecting to be abused & not ever disappointed
Tears falling on my black belly are cool mean nothing
I've been in this pit so often just when I think I've
finally done enough work to be free
I find his penis in my throat I can't breathe it's back
into the darkness for three hours or five
Yes I survived but why

My face is wet with grief what's new
I lay awake four hours the other night
plotting to the smallest detail how to kill him
I could strangle her this morning when she says she loves me
He said it too
Sex is a minefield warfare sex is the hole where pleasure
means losing face
I can't walk today   lay on my bed shrieking my fist
into the wall   wanting to make a wound as big as this one
in me   These words got me out
You can grab on too if you need them

for MORGAN AHERN

LEAF BEHIND MY EAR

pale pink rosebuds near my arms
light catches refracts a glitter of dawn
Nakai's flute prays beside our pile of warm quilts
our legs entwined
A question a woman asked me once
floats upward in my fingers
How do you have hope to go on?
Poplar leaves brought from italy years ago shimmer dance
surrounding our lazy morning
the quiet pine sways with wispy needles
I can't answer that question I've carried with me
except to say   *I'm alive   I'm loved*
there's work to do

November 7, 1990

INSIDE

white words prison bars wall too thick I shape
my spirit near water's edge
Hidden hands in the dark reach back for wild grasses
I'm weaving a strong basket to carry myself
These words are ash these words are shards
which cut hollow hoarse heavy
This is a table but I don't want it
This is a floor but I prefer the dirt
These are windows but I want wind
How many Indians can dance on the heads of civilization pins?
Shadows summon me   My head echoes
with nonsense I've memorized to stay alive
Aching confetti go on the wind
Silence comes like dawn a blessing a watching of dark eyes
caught in the light
See this basket   tight   safe
I'm throwing everything out of it
to make more room for us
Look! These little words
dance around nosy & noisy   Here they go!
Floating toward snowy mountains
where they'll melt
white into white

for JOY HARJO

THOSE TEARS

of a white woman who came to the group for Women of Color
only
her grief cut us into guilt while we clutched the straw
of this tiny square inch we have which we need
so desperately when we need so much more
We talked her into leaving
which took 10 minutes of our precious 60
Those legion white Lesbians whose feelings are hurt
because we have a Lesbians of Color Potluck
once a month for 2 hours
without them
Those tears of the straight woman
because we kicked out her boyfriend at the Lesbians only
poetry reading where no microphone was provided
& the room was much too small for all of us
shouting that we were imperialists
though I had spent 8 minutes trying to explain
to her that an oppressed people
cannot oppress their oppressor
She ignored me
charged into the room weeping & storming
taking up 9 minutes of our precious tiny square inch
Ah those tears
which could be jails, graves, rapists, thieves, thugs
those tears which are so puffed up with inappropriate grief
Those women who are used to having their tears work
rage at us
when they don't
We are not real Feminists they say
We do not love women
I yell back with a wet face
Where are our jobs?   Our apartments?
Our voices in parliament or congress?
Where is our safety from beatings, from murder?
You cannot even respect us to allow us
60 uninterrupted minutes for ourselves

Your tears are chains
Feminism is the right of each woman
to claim her own life her own time
her own uninterrupted 60 hours
                            60 days
                            60 years
No matter how sensitive you are
if you are white
you are
No matter how sensitive you are
if you are a man
you are
We who are not allowed to speak have the right
to define our terms our turf
These facts are not debatable
Give us our inch
& we'll hand you a hanky

for MAV & DENISE, who guarded the door after the incident at the Lesbian reading &
   thus, didn't get to hear the poetry

WHEN I LOVED YOU AS A JEW

I knew I wouldn't have to explain genocide
or open your heart to my life
We were not strangers but warriors of different clans
enriched & conspiring
I've loved you for your fierce clarity your insistence
on justice in a world stony with lies pretense denial
ignorance
I've loved you in marches at rallies in meetings
in darkened theatres   beside water & in mountains
We've fought ardently warring & laughing & weeping our way
to this hot afternoon in someone else's bed far from home
where I love you for the puddles under our asses
your head lazy on my shoulder
your arm across my belly   breasts pressed to my hips
your breathing an airy drum   your hair stuck to my shoulder
every cell in our bodies good   every pulse holy
every pore a lake of peace   our skin damp & dreaming
this moment of stillness
which has never been obscene

for ILENE SAMOWITZ

Heart of the Matter — Her Old Love Charm

YOU COME

into my throat with a surge of spring thrusting
into sky hot alive with clouds racing as my heart
into the moon beats silver going over
into the sun lively with our laughter   sly glances
Into my sea you are a dragon flying on fire
breathing slow & simple our fingers tremble green & new
into deepest roots going down below the rocks
into core of lava where life begins a small child turns
into you this woman raw with life alive beating
into that dark tunnel of your childhood I call
into your heart you are blue & green & ruby & gold
Into your lungs I blow a calm warm breeze
Into your hands I plant everything you love to eat & roses
Into your feet I kiss a dance
Into your eyes I unveil this rising phoenix
Into a never dead girl
I lift you
into wide eons of night send you breathing
into stars

for KITTY TSUI

WHERE YOU STOOD

winds blow fierce   Sheer cliff of our vicious end
In my heart your name is empty   Howling trees whip
I'm carefully erasing the bruises of your sea color eyes
I'm unbraiding your harsh mouth from my hair
Your smell washed from my sheets I don't remember the shape
of your breasts or the pulse of our need
Watch this high tide obliterate
our life   our years   our promises
our terrible fights
You loomed large in my landscape   See
how erosion has taken you
worn you out of me
Where you stood   Look now at all the time which cradles
me gently   Your bamboo laughter breaks in distant ears
Your songs silently eat themselves
I wash my face in tears   I wash my hands in new love
I wash out
this place where you stood   Wind comes up
My hair whips my eyes dry
When they ask after you I say
Who?

I'M BURNING UP

my need to be loved by others, which prevents me from learning to love myself   One thing & another, I wasn't my mother's joyous gift, but her frightening burden   As is the way with infant crea- tures, I tried to win her affection & approval for my survival   I lost

Now, frantic for affection from others, I'm unable to engage my thinking self   I madly desire anyone to like me, even when I don't like them   Stuffing them down me in an obscene parody of relationship   Because I serve so many bosses, my actions are random, unclear, unsensible, often cruel   My terror, which was my mother's legacy (which she in turn received from her mother), causes me to be needy, unreliable, giving away so much of myself that I feel the wind blowing through my belly   I become resentful because there can never be enough approval, I'm never satisfied No one can love me in the way I needed my mother to do   That wound increases in size, gobbles me up, runs me as the years flee

I alternately hate her empty hands & pity her for them   I've made myself strong enough to look at us—but I can't give her my strength   My mother's goal is for me to prove I love *her*   To nurture her as penance for my grandmother's coldness, my father's cruelty, because I am the oldest, it is my duty   She is frozen in her need, can't admit it   Can't think of how she could change her life herself to meet those needs   She begins to understand my strength & insight into our situation, so she clings to me, demands emotional care-taking & reassurance, at the exact juncture when I feel most angry about how she neglected me   Do you hear the whine in the word "neglect," which shames me & causes me to want to erase myself?   As the one with the most skills for emotional honesty, I owe it to her to be gentle, loving, forgiving   But where is my anger to go?   She has buried hers toward her mother   When I was a helpless child (is that a redundant phrase?), she vented that anger on me in continual emotional & physical beatings   She has now erased that aspect of our history   I've become cruel because I want distance from her, won't take care of her (while fighting mountains of guilt in myself because of it)   Can I allow her to erase our history?   She is desperate for my pretense that she was a good mother   I am desperate for her acknowledgment that my childhood was a painful chaos of beatings & her emotional absence   I understand, from a feminist viewpoint (poverty, my father's indifference, her own terror), why she behaved as she did—but I can't forgive her as long as she denies my reality

I sometimes feel as though the only emotional trick that she has left up her sleeve, is to die   I know I'll be inconsolable then   All the grief will flood me because it will finally be safe to feel it   She won't be there to deny it, mock it, trivialize it   The whole tortured knot of our connection will unravel

I have to face this chasm   She has never known me because she doesn't know herself   I'm a figment of her sentimental guilt Her passion for declaring her love for me, now (which she didn't do when I was a child or young adult), is 40 years too late, isn't even love   It is desperation   She wants me to comfort her before she dies   To agree to erasure   To love her for wanting to erase me

My Lesbianism is an unpleasant aberration which we don't mention   She "loves me anyway"   She doesn't want honest answers when she asks about my life (so that I will ask her about hers, which is the actual point of the call)   She wants chatty cathy piping up   *I'm fine Mom. How are you. I love you. You're the best Mom ever.*   I wish they'd manufacture one   I'd send it back & forth on airplanes, dressed just as she'd like me to dress, for family gatherings   We'd both be a lot happier   A walk on the beach by myself in a storm is more comforting than any interaction between my mother & me   At least she no longer asks me about marriage   Probably because she really doesn't like the grandchildren she already has, although she'd deny that, as she does everything else They're loud, they break things, they're messy, they don't behave themselves, they wear her out   Nothing's changed

I frighten my mother   I'm the cruel, mysterious, unreliable child   I was in therapy & nuthouses for years because I was the problem   When I moved 750 miles away, I began to heal   I've concealed my healing from her because I suspect she would try to destroy it   Not viciously   But because it places me outside her grasp

As I refuse to take care of my mother emotionally—*consciously*, not simply with my old tricks of avoidance—I begin to refuse other unreasonable demands   Everybody wants the good mother they didn't have because their mother was trying to be a person with a boot in her back   I've been the good mother to my lovers to get love   I want to be the child I've had to deny   So I can finally grow up   I want to create a self, as I've endlessly created love affairs   I want to give attention to myself   I understand that this is "childish, infantile"   But if I don't give this to myself, I'll remain covertly & irresponsibly childish   Like my mother   My first priority must be my own healing   Otherwise, all my attempts at relationship are doomed

I've been avoiding her calls again   I didn't send them an anniversary present or extravagant flowers (as in the past) or even a card   I have been appeasing her, kissing her ass all of my life   I thought I would die if I didn't   I'm terrified as I attempt to pull away from her now   Can't you see the sky falling

I don't love her   I don't even like her   I pity her misery   I hate myself for not loving her   I should wear elevator shoes so I could rise above   I want to find my way to love & work & balance & forgiveness & I don't want to stop to show her how   She doesn't want to know anyway or we wouldn't be in this tar pit   Her goal is to find a pink cloud that will finally work   I want to abandon her to her own devices   That's no way for a daughter to act

WEEDING

my garden in Autumn I want to send you this wind
dancing through Madronas
Alder trees going gold
Sun piercing fog as the buoy sings her bells
These two Geese going south who cause me to pause
root in muddy hands
for their hoarse calls to everybody else
as they circle over the sound
This heat soothing my sweaty shoulders
smell of Lavender I've gathered for winter letters
This Birch who brings me home
moment of no walls no locks no guards no torture
no lonely cruel years
These two Apples
not quite ready to pick
who hang pale yellow blushed in dapples
They're the only ones & the first to grow
after years of tent caterpillar infestations
I refused to spray with poison
I planted this tree about the time they locked you up
Next year I pray for a better crop
& you
biting into one
on your way
to visit your mother
or go fishing
anyplace you can smell the wind

for Leonard Peltier

DEATH TAKES

you from my eyes like falling thousands of feet to rocks below
or a barred window facing a concrete wall
Takes you from my eyes though not my heart
where you murmur in odd moments until that beast
grief bites down hard   I'm breathless nose running
As I eat crab   I'm eating for you
As I write you're on the couch with your feet up
an eyebrow raised to make sure   I get it right
Your hands were inside me you pulse through my veins now
reaching to stir garlic butter I know
that love weaves continuous after breathing stops
past hospital beds   other lovers
the rage we broke against each other's bodies
Death is a cruel knife without respite
if I could believe your soul continues in more
than these memories in my arms
consolation might soothe this ache   As it is
I don't know what death means
accept that plainly
Taken from my ears
your rich laughter is a morning web I brush past
Gone   from my air   my plate is empty
though here in my heart you're safe from america at last
beating your drum on fire

for PAT

LESBIAN AIR

She burns her mouth aches for the taste of Cunt unmistakable smell
on her hands cherished in public places for she refuses to wash it
off   She dreams her hands are branded Dyke by the government
     Instead of wearing gloves of shame she waves her hands to
everyone laughing until she cracks into tears as they slam shut their
faces   She is disgusting they say   Some of them   Enough to
bring her to her knees in despair   She doesn't stay there long
Up again to water the Lesbian garden   mend the Lesbian ramp
wash the Lesbian breakfast dishes   Her work to make money is a
mindless stew of misery, her actions sometimes wrong, her beliefs
sometimes inaccurate but it is clear that licking Cunt is always good
always right always holy   She is a fisheater they say whipped by
cats she is at the mercy of her tongue her fingers   She chooses each
moment to love women to side with the Dykes to take the heat to be a
Lesbian even when other Lesbians refuse her as too radical too
frightening too much   There cannot be too much   Abundance is
the love of our mother whose breast we plant   whose eyes we bless
     Ah the theory of Lesbianism is a lot of words that not all Lesbians
understand or want to   It is the wanting of women we share
parting of forbidden roses   Our tongues meet we can never have
too much of each other as we speak on palestinian land rights, as we
march against racism, as we demand abortion rights for women who
might hate us as we stand for them, as we wheel, as we follow night
into day as we breathe Lesbian air, plant Lesbian sunflowers &
carrots, as we train Lesbian horses, as we write Lesbian traffic tickets,
as we predict Lesbian earthquakes, as we repair Lesbian cars, as we
hold jobs from Lesbian wheelchairs, as we swim in Lesbian lakes with
the loons, as we care for the wounded & dying our tender Lesbian
hands nurture life   We bring babies here we bring paintings here
we bring poetry and song here   We bring Lesbian joy into the
wintery lives of the lonely   We are our mother's infinite variety

We are Lesbian redwoods   We are Lesbian rain forests   we are
Lesbian rock formations   we are Lesbian canyons   we are
Lesbian desert pines   we are Lesbian lizards   we are the sea of
Lesbians the breathing wind of Lesbians we are the falling cherry
petals of Lesbians we are the Lesbian moon rising full of our fallen
warriors' songs   we are the Lesbian sky

for JEWELLE GOMEZ

ON A SHORE FAR FROM YOURS

blue jade waves come ceaseless as change
throbbing life & death foam of our desire
to name mystery we barely see
to still this water which surges past our fear
to hold on to some weed of certainty
as we carry within us this moving motion
of recede   advance   recede
no more sensible & as beautifull
as a tidepool of anemones
whose soft green & white tentacles
echo our need

for AUDRE LORDE

THE OKEYDOEKEY TRIBE

Historically these people have been noted for a strange dish called hamburgers, which contain no ham. They also contain no burgers, a simile for storekeepers, although many salespeople might be better ground up, especially the kind that sell to Indians at higher prices or not at all.

The Okeydoekey tribe has one of the widest ranging territories of any group known to man. They are very similar in this respect to cockroaches, ants & rats, all of whom have an identical widespread distribution. There has been much speculation about the method of their dispersal, but the currently accepted theory is that they made such a mess wherever they went that they were in constant need of new territory. Rumor has it that they plan to colonize outer space if they can find any place with enough resources to sell.

They celebrate all major occasions with a liquid distilled from rotted fruit or vegetables. They consume as much of this as they can in an effort to be happy. This often fails. They do not seem to have any other method of enjoying themselves. Some members have stopped using this liquid, as they find it disagreeable & go to meetings to talk about it instead.

The Okeydoekey people will, in fact, meet for almost any excuse & will often argue long into the night about who should speak first or what shape the table they sit at must be. We have long been puzzled by the importance of the table but apparently this is closely guarded information, as none of our informants could offer a clue.

We have found that when attempting to communicate with the Okeydoekey people, who are, as a general rule, very primitive, that it is best to offer money first, as this is their abiding love & concern. We recommend large amounts of cash before any independent inquiry is conducted into their habits.

for JENNIE & JIM VANDER WALL

SESTINA FOR ILENE

Taking you my fist becomes a rose
opening into our journey where wings
move over deep water dark with my tongue curling
into your screaming joy your flushed red breasts
Trail of crimson petals I paint along your throat
Your thighs clench my head until I'm near the edge

of losing breath flying into this dawning edge
where our hearts pound one drum Our bed a rose
As I open my eyes drift slow   your throat
flutters alive dancing hungry with bright wings
My free hand reaches to stroke your breast
My cheeks wet with your dark hair curling

I'm open to your scarlet openness curling
through my veins   Our bodies blurred no edge
to cut our tongues   My heart dark within my breast
Our fingers twine   My lips suckle your nipples rose
Air soft with songs of our flushed wings
as joy moves deeply red in my humming throat

You suck my toes dancing my throat
open   White water heats rushes through my curling
blood   My thighs tremble open Touch wings
of your tongue as you fling me into this edge
of silken red flowers blurring to rose
I gasp   Squeeze my dancing breasts

My mouth desperate hot to suck your breast
I find you deep growling in the dark your throat
painting inside my skin with roses
My eyes wet petals   My fingers curling
as you lift my ass & enter me edge
to edge so deep I find my hungry wings

soaring out my love clenches & rises wings
behind my back opening in my breast
reaching joy thick & drifting to an edge
of losing walls   All my cries pulsing open throated
Deep inside my hungry petals curling
around your hand which must be a rose

Our thighs rose   Wildly throbbing our throats
still sing our wet breasts   Our spirits curling
deep within our dancing edges where we are all wings

for ILENE SAMOWITZ

DOWN

into the dark bloody grave of war
we're dragged by men we've never met or touched
speaking laundry language
Below their clean sweeps   successful missions
are the bodies of women   children   men   our neighbors
on the other side of the world
Screams of death echo our names
as we admire a lovely sunset over the lake
not speaking of the bombing raids we've just protested
Our voices hoarse as we surged down streets
stretching as far as we could see
A young man struck out at me as we passed
as though to stab my belly
his eyes boiling with hate
I'm marching for him   for his life
which probably won't survive ground combat
in a desert land he cannot comprehend
The government lies   the media obscures our numbers
Deeply ashamed for what the dawn will bring I ask
How many are dying
from the taxes I've paid
with my tired hands?

for the IRAQI AND KUWAITI PEOPLE

MORNING SONG

It wasn't until the radio said
that you had surrendered
that I knew how desperately I needed you to go on
to be the unraveling edge who would change our lives
though I'm too afraid to stand with a rifle at a barricade
did nothing to help but worry, pray, admire & send money
Tonight the moon is a heavy half
hanging over the water with a sorry face
like the effigies they made of us
Younger I fought fiercely with more than words
I had it beaten & kicked out of me
warped by clanging metal doors with many locks
Time has brought me to my knees more coward than I can stand
I felt myself begin to rise with the first news
of you so far away so brave so sure
I guess this means maybe
we'll have another golf course after all
I can hear the long screams of the bulldozers
they love to rape our mother with
I can see the piles of what they call brush
but we call Life
burning in a fire that keeps no one warm   cooks nothing
in a crazy blaze of their hatred whose smoke coats our lungs
These tears are private frightened gestures of a woman
who cannot stand guns & death & how useless
they think our lives are
how easily they'll kill us   how much they want to
even though they have golf courses all over the world
I weep because we are alone with this heaviness
our knees on fire
Sending my spirit to you I try to remember that we've never
surrendered
We've only said so
to survive

for DONNA GOODLEAF, BETH BRANT, AMANDA WHITE & the MOHAWK NATION

EARS TO THE HEART OF THE WIND

we're going on an Appaloosa of feathers
for a long ride where fences can't go
to talk with Crows   Gulls   Geese
up in the belly velvet air
Listening for the hooves in our hearts
Wind embraces this high lark
above feather tree tops caressing sky
This Horse has paisley swirls of breath
crystal in the fog
This is a black wet silk rainy night horse
This is a dawn satin pony
whose rump is dappled with stars
We're prancing   Ears crisp in autumn roar
on this downy ride   Tender face of wings
We're watching for the hooves of the story
high in pearl gray wind
Birds brush our backs
We're going dancing with Joy

for the QUILEUTE NATION

URBAN INDIAN

Steeling myself in the steel gray skies of skyscrapers
my feet are so hungry for an unexpected flower
flash of fur or feathers   for a path that breathes
not this poisonous gas concrete men tied up in ties
vying with each other to cheat steal abuse
chewing the fat full of hatred for life
which lives unpredictable   deeply mysterious
on the edge of their hard edge photo realism reality

It is evening the Moon is rising slowly
I drum an old song on the hood of an abandoned stripped car
singing so softly only the stars hear
calling down horses   calling down deer   calling down loons
calling down turtles
while the sky flushes lavender   mist rises blue
Everywhere the roads crumble
as green our mother takes herself back   fine dust is all
that's left of these prisons & pain
I am dreaming on this
Dream on with me

for DENNIS BANKS

PERTINENT ADDRESSES

Send donations for information:

Support for Future Generations
(Big Mountain resistance)
Box 22134
Flagstaff, AZ   86002
U.S.A.

Leonard Peltier Defense
Box 583
Lawrence, KS   66044
U.S.A.

Chief Ruby Denton (Stein Forest)
Lytton & Mount Currie Bands
Box 1420
Lillooet, B.C.   V0K 1V0
Canada

For Music:

Floyd Westerman Tapes
Red Crow Productions
Box 4160
Malibu, CA   90265
U.S.A.

R. Carlos Nakai Tapes
Celestial Harmonies
Box 30122
Tucson, AZ   85751
U.S.A.

Gay & Lesbian Native Organizations:

American Indian Gays & Lesbians
Box 10229
Minneapolis, MN   55458-3229
U.S.A.

Gay American Indians
phone (415) 621-4716
1347 Divisadero, #312
San Francisco, CA   94115
U.S.A.

Gays & Lesbians of First Nations
Box 56, 684 Yonge St.
Toronto, ON   M4Y 2A6
Canada

Nichiwakan N.G.S.
phone (204) 772-3606
616 Broadway Ave.
Winnipeg, MB   R3C 0W8
Canada

WeWah BarCheAmpe
New York City
phone (212) 765-2927

Author Biography

Born Nov. 7, 1946 off reservation in San Francisco of a Menominee father & a Lithuanian / Alsace-Lorraine mother
Self-educated   Artist as well as writer
Author of *Not Vanishing* & contributor to many anthologies, including: *This Bridge Called My Back; A Gathering of Spirit; Gay & Lesbian Poetry of Our Time; Intricate Passions; Making Face, Making Soul / Haciendo Caras; Dancing on the Rim of the World & Living the Spirit*
Indigenous Land & Treaty Rights Activist, working for the freedom of Leonard Peltier, the Diné Nation at Big Mountain, the Mohawk Nation at Kanehsatake & various other Native Rights causes
Proud Lesbian for 25 years, this coming May
Loving Tia to 6 nieces & nephews
Sober since October, 1988
Make words, not war!

Reviewers praise *Not Vanishing*, Chrystos' first book of poetry/prose

"In reading the poems of Chrystos I sense a struggle to return to music: the music of Native American ritual singing. And while her work deals with the most modern circumstances... it is the ancient, urgent voice of tribal ritual that gives her work the punch that takes my breath away."

—Jewelle Gomez
Trivia

" ...to walk the streets as a Native American, a lesbian, a woman, to live against the racism, misogyny and homophobia which destroys the soul, it is of this which Chrystos writes, with a clarity and fury which demands to be heard."

—Tamai Kobayashi
Canadian Book Review Annual

"The range of her issues goes far beyond the singular idea of lesbian love, for we are all serenaded, wooed, cajoled, tickled, schemed into an ultimate surrender to her enticing poetics."

—Marie Annharte Baker
Zajets

"If Chrystos were a less skilled poet, she might be content to voice her outrage and leave us with her words ringing in our ears. Yet there is a message of hope: winding its way through the book are lyrical love poems, surfacing in unlikely places, often following poem after poem of despair and outrage."

—Andrea Lerner
Western American Literature

"Chrystos' poems reach out across the page: skeins of geese patterning the white sky... Her work is not just accurate and topical. It is also risky and original and beautiful, gentle and surprising."

—Christian McEwen
City Limits

"This volume is a must read—one shocking, electrifying, defiant, mesmerizing poem after another."

—Rebecca Johns
Guardian Book Review Supplement

Press Gang Publishers Feminist Co-operative is committed to publishing a wide range of writing by women which explores themes of personal and political struggles for equality.

A free listing of our books is available from:
Press Gang Publishers, 603 Powell Street, Vancouver, B.C. V6A 1H2 Canada